Sounds of Burned Silence

Sequel to Virgin to the Life

John Collins

LET'S RETHINK THAT

ATLANTA, GA

www.letsrethinkthat.com

You may contact John Collins at:
johncollins280@gmail.com
Twitter: authorjohncollins
Instagram: princeofpages

Sounds of Burned Silence Copyright © 2014

.

Dedication

This is dedicated to anyone who's ever felt powerless against the person behind judgments fueled by hate-filled words but eventually finding the courage to use their voice to burn through the paralyzing fear silence can bring

Table of Contents

Facial Showers

This fool gave me something that can kill me! Foreign bodies playing romp a damn room throughout every crevice of my once healthy body. I tuned every other word my doctor said out and was stuck somewhere in my full Detroit mind hearing *Mr. Williams, unfortunately you tested positive,* and wanting to yell out, *WHAT THE FUCK DID YOU JUST SAY TO ME?!* In my mind, the frame-by-frame view of Gary and his ex-screwing in a LaQuinta Inn live on our HD T.V. set fire to my rage! And brought me to this place...

I sat there staring at my doctor with tunnel vision while he babbled on and on throwing out words and phrases resembling counseling, support groups, and making healthy safe sex choices. I was not trying to absorb any of that. The only thing on my mind was an immense desire to walk up to that smooth talking, sexy, 6'1," Bahamian, caramel complexioned boyfriend of mine and do something I am not a fan of... *KICK HIM STIFF SQUARE IN THE NUTS* with a deep treaded steel toe boot and the agility of an Ostrich.

I am not sure how I was able to keep my cool and walk out of the doctor's office without saying so much as two words. I didn't know what to say. It seemed as if everyone was looking at me funny or whispering about me. I avoided eye contact; I couldn't help but feel like they knew my business... what that

1

lying, trifling ass Gary had done to me!!!...what he has done to us!!!

Once I finished checking out of the facility, I zipped down the hall towards the elevators with Gary on my mind and papers in hand. This is someone whom I love... my first everything?!?!?! I shared a life with this man! Hell! I trusted this man with my life in more than a literal sense, and he plays with not only his but mine and breaks up our happy home. I was livid -scared beyond belief. I couldn't get to the car fast enough. I felt like I needed to be in an environment familiar to me so that I could calm down. The sounds of the outside world were somehow amplified and overwhelming. I quickly pulled my keys out of my pocket and pressed the button to unlock the door while taking a quick look behind me.

Once I sat inside and closed the door, I let my body mold itself into the seat. I rolled up the left sleeve of my sweater and ran my finger across the tape and gauze irritating my skin, yet covering the needle pricks from my blood draw. I scratched around the tape and panicked for some reason when my finger caught a corner of the bandage. I smooth it back down not wanting anything else to enter my body. I rolled my sleeve back down as my phone rang. I reached for it observing the name on the caller I.D. I took a deep breath and answered...

"Jason?"

"What!" I barked before taking a second-deep

cleansing breath.

"Baby, I'm glad you picked up the phone. You okay?"

"Nope," I said trying to control my breathing.

"I guess that was a stupid question?"

"Not really."

"Can we talk, babes?"

"No, but you can talk to a doctor."

"Huh?"

"You can talk to a doctor about these test results I'm holding in my hand because of you," I said still trying to keep my cool. As much as I wanted too, I wasn't trying to get into a shouting match.

"What? What you mean by that?"

"You need to go get checked out. Take your ex with you too, you dirty dick bastards," I said in a very nasty tone.

"Baby, I truly apologize for all of this," he replied. The sad part is, I could hear the sincerity and hurt in his voice. However, I wasn't quite ready to forgive just yet....

"Dude, save it! Not only have you broken my heart, but you gave me...Go see a doctor!" I said hanging up the phone abruptly.

It felt like the entire world had left me. I kept trying to figure out what I did wrong in this situation to deserve not only being cheated on, but also getting this type of news? How could a thing so sweet turn so sour like it never even had a flavor palatable to ingest?

I didn't want to go to my friends and talk with them about it, and this wasn't a matter I could discuss with my parents although I really needed them. DAMN!!!!! FUCK!!!! Everyone can always count on Jason to do the right thing, be the shoulder and sounding board, keep his mouth closed, to not rock the boat, to not hold them accountable to their own compunctions, but what about me!?!?! Who's here for me!?!?!

I made up my mind not to hold back anymore. Something changed and tarnished the trust I wanted so desperately to believe was there in people. If the love of my life can do me like this, then I know what they mean now when they say, the world doesn't give a fuck about you. This feeling, this revelation not only made sense, but it changed something inside of me. How could a person like me with so much love for the world have the world kick him in the gut repeatedly by the society he lives in, the uniform he proudly wore, the parents and family he was blessed with, and then his first love?

I tried to hold back my tears because I don't like to allow myself to cry, and I had released enough of them. Maybe I have done enough of it? Was I overdue for a good cry? I was snapped out of my thoughts when the piercing sound of a toddler crying caused me to jump. I wiped my face and avoided eye contact with the woman parked in front of me. I placed the key in the ignition, started the engine, and made my way out of the parking deck with tears streaming down my face. I could not stop them and there was no need too. They were coming down with such heft; they didn't have time to pool and blur my vision. The mix of confusion and anger my mind was enthralled with was over abundant.

I was a wet angry mess, and before I knew it, I had made my way down the street on which Gary and I lived... out of habit... I guess. My palms became sweaty, and I could feel my teeth gnashing in the midst of my anger as I approached our driveway. I stopped the car in the middle of the street looking over at the entrance debating on whether or not to pull into the driveway. I closed my eyes and felt all of the hurt, jealousy, and betrayal start to get the best of me. My breathing and heartbeat were competing with one another as if there were some finish line to cross. My body temperature increased causing me to perspire. I whispered the Lord's name and was suddenly startled by the sound of a loud lingering car horn.

That was just the sign I needed. It was clear as day what I needed to do... move on, but how? I didn't know how... especially without Gary who left me to deal with this shit he gave me. I drove around the city not sobbing but crying uncontrollably trying to figure out how this void was going to be filled. Trying to figure out how my health was going to be affected moving forward. Trying to figure out, why the hell the sun was shining causing the weather to be a direct contradiction to the stormy precipitation life itself had sent through my tear ducts. I threw on a pair of dark sunglasses to shield my eyes from the brightness making its way in through the windshield. I couldn't enjoy its warmth and beauty today as I made it back to my hotel room. I was in a state of dissolution wanting so bad to do like I have in the past when things got the best of me and suck it up, but this was a hurt beyond anything I'd experienced before. I thought my Daddy labeling me his second daughter was the pinnacle of pain, but that seemed like a kiss on the cheek compared to this. That was the only other time in my life a man has made me cry, but not like this.

I parked the car, took pause to stop the flow of lament, grabbed my belongings, and quickly made my way down the walkway parallel to the building. I tripped through the entrance of the hotel lobby calling attention to myself, and falling to the floor as if someone behind me had pushed me. The force of the fall sent my sunglasses sliding to the left of me, my knap sack up and around my shoulders, and the papers in my right hand from the doctor's office spiraling to the floor next to the feet of a well-dressed businessman conversing with the Concierge.

I panicked and quickly shuffled over to snatch the papers up as he began to bend down to pick them up for me. I didn't want him reading the markings embossed on them. I ignored the two of them asking if I was okay and if I needed help. I gathered my documents and returned the shades to my face making an abrupt B-line to the stairwell to avoid further contact with anyone.

I ran up the four flights of stairs to my room trying to contain my emotions. Out of breath and on the verge of sobbing, I clumsily shoved the key card into the slot, swung the door open and rushed to the bathroom to get a glimpse of myself in the mirror. I stood there in the dark for about five minutes studying my silhouette and focusing on the whites of my eyes catching the muted light making its appearance into the confines of the restroom. I was scared I wouldn't recognize myself but made the conscious decision to turn the lights on so that I could face my current reality for the first time in solitude. The flicker of fluorescent lights coming on caused me to wince as my eyes adjusted to their brilliance. I was clutching the notes from the doctor in my right hand, remembering verbatim what the words printed on them said. I felt violated. What did I do to deserve this? Did the homophobes now have the satisfaction of being right and proving me wrong? Was this punishment for going against the so called natural order of things? I couldn't draw a conclusion to the depth of agony I was feeling, let alone develop an answer to these questions. I could only answer the hows associated with my tear stained face and puffy blood shot eyes.

Facial Showers

I ran my hands across my cheeks taking note of the gritty residue left behind from the previous flow of emotions running down my face. I now had to accept abandonment from Gary. First, my family does it and now my man? I thought to myself, who are you going to take away from me next, Lord? This was truly unfair because now all I had to look forward too was doctor's visits and the possibility of never trusting another dude again. I needed the comfort of darkness right now. I wanted nothing more but God, my thoughts, and myself.

I turned the lights off and drew the drapes closed, stripped down to my underwear, and curled up under the covers of the soft bedding, letting its coolness surround and embrace my body. The subtle aroma of lavender infused sheets slightly calmed my mood. I closed my eyes as the ticking of my watch put me in a trance of happier times with the two of us laughing, going on late night runs together, me cooking his favorite meals, date nights, him asking how the day treated me, him looking sexy as hell getting out of the shower in the morning dripping water all over the floor.

I would scold him about this and he would shut me up by wrapping his strong arms around me, still wet, and kiss me like he hadn't seen me in months. He wouldn't say a word, but simply claim what was his. He would always make me feel special and free from danger until the idea of us making love brought me back to the present current events surrounding my life.

Thoughts of my once warm vanilla scented happy home was replaced by the cold medicinal scented sterile environment of the clinic I had just left. The deep rugged baritone of my Nubian King whispering sweet words of encouragement and kindness in my ear were replaced by the sound of the authoritative abrupt pitch of that Caucasian doctor of mine revealing alarming results and the harsh reality of a love gone wrong. The sweet taste of my man's dick I remember oh so well on my tongue was replaced by the thought of a bland tasting latex condom found in a white bag provided by the Chicago Public Health Department.

The intimacy, closeness, and deep stroke only Gary could provide me as he reinforced the love he had for me with each vigorous thrust of his erect shaft between my firm mounds of pleasure and tight inviting hole would truly be missed. Gary and I were a done deal. He had taken so many things from me that I had no idea how to get back, namely my heart.

I was lost in love, still in love, and out of love at the same time. I was no longer the vibrant innocent virgin to the life, but rather a precocious extension of my previous self. Maybe life wasn't the romanticized, free spirited, unbridled image I had developed in my head. Maybe it was time for me to stop living in my head and protect myself not only physically, but emotionally as well. My approach to life now would stem from a visceral standpoint. In spite of it all though, I still believed in love simply because I am love...

Results in a Fight

When I finally got it together and decided I was ready to face Gary without going to prison, I called him one evening and told him I'd like for us to talk. However, that same night, I learned that my once-upon-a-time almost boo Darius was home on Rest and Relaxation leave for a brief stint from his military tour in Kuwait. I completely forgot all about Gary and our issues and dropped everything to see him. Everything with Darius always seemed to be so coincidental. It was as if he was always there to watch over me. My very own black Incredible Hulk.

I remembered how beautiful he looked to me that night. It was as if I was seeing him for the first time. Everything about him was perfect in my eyes. From his smooth hairless dark skin, the way he kept his hair in a low brush cut, to his solid exquisitely thick muscular build. He stood 5'11, and was very mannish. He was such a man about everything from the way he ate to his baggy attire. He used to turn me on every time I saw him, but we were just cool. The laughs never stopped because we were constantly joking around and teasing each other. He took care of me that evening and that next morning I awoke with Darius still lying on top of me as if he were a blanket safeguarding me from the cold. He looked so peaceful and comfortable which calmed my restless and confused spirit. He made me begin to feel trust again all because of what had happened the night before...

Darius had convinced me to go clubbing with him and I decided to forget about Gary and hang out with him and my best friends, Shawn, Michael, and Preston. I thought about how much I really wanted Darius that night. I just didn't want to confuse my desire for him with my wanting to get back at Gary for his infidelity and the consequences that came with it. It would have complicated things and changed the dynamic of our friendship. Due to the circumstances, I was glad we couldn't go all the way because I know I would have more than likely given in to his advances.

We walked off of the dance floor. I was holding on to the pockets of his jeans guiding the way as he held a firm grip on my waist. I didn't know what was going to happen once we got back to his room, but whatever it was, I made up in my mind that I was going to try my best to say no.

I spotted Shawn posted up talking to his new boyfriend Andre, better known as Gary's best friend, at the back of the club. Michael was talking to some thick chocolate boy close to Shawn and Andre. Darius and I walked over to Michael. I tapped him on the shoulder and told him we were about to head out. He gave me this sly look and whispered in my ear to wrap it up. I know what ya'll about to do. Here's a golden ticket. We shared a laugh as he pressed a condom into the palm of my hand. I discreetly placed it into my pocket and proceeded to walk over to speak with

Shawn as   Darius and Michael exchanged a few words. Preston was nowhere to be found, so I figured I'd text him goodbye.

In the middle of our conversation, I was caught off guard when I felt Darius walk up behind me and hug me. He whispered in my ear, "Let's leave." I turned toward him and smiled. He let me go and once again took his place behind me. I looked back up at him as we started walking towards the entrance. I turned around to face forward and saw Gary storming his way through the crowd. Suddenly, my whole demeanor changed as we locked eyes. I stopped dead in my tracks. Darius asked what was wrong and that's when things escalated. I could feel the warmth of his breath surround the nape of my neck as the little hairs began to raise like that of a frightened kitten. Gary walked right up to me and got all in my face. I felt Darius's muscles tense up before he let my body go.

"What the fuck! I'm waiting on you to come home, so we can talk and you up in this bitch sluttin' yo' self out for this nigga!" he shouted gesturing towards Darius in a disrespectful manner.

"Gary, I know one thing you'd better calm down. Don't be talking to me like I'm your child. Who the hell do you think you are?" I said tapping him in the chest with my middle finger.

"Yo' mothafuckin' nigga, got-damn it! What the fuck is you thinking Jason?" he said beating his chest with one hand and grabbing mine with the other.

"You been missing in action almost three fucking weeks and I gotta hear from my boy that you shaking your ass in a club! What the fuck is that shit about?" he said. I got up in his face. There was a crowd forming around us and I saw Michael out the corner of my eye approach the three of us.

"Don't come up in here raising your voice and cursing at me like you own me, punk! If you kept your dick in your pants, then you wouldn't be sitting at home alone," I paused and took a breath and then smirked. "So what you hurt now?" I said sizing him up. The alcohol made me feel brave all of a sudden. "You know I said it before, but I mean it this time. Go to hell! I ain't gotta deal with this madness. You ain't about to embarrass me in front of all these punks tonight," I said as I pushed him out of my way.

Gary grabbed my arm and pulled me back in front of him. Darius stepped in front of me and put some space in-between the two of us.

"Yo', my man, on the real, I'ma need you to bring this shit down a couple notches. Neither one of ya'll are in the right frame of mind to talk right now. So let's dead this shit before they call the police. Now I'm asking nicely, bruh. A'ight?" he said looking Gary right square in the eye.

"Nigga, if you don't get up outta my face! This ain't got shit to do with your bitch ass!" he said, directing his attention back at me.

"Jason, let's leave okay. Before this gets ugly,"

Michael said to me tugging on my arm.

"Jason, let's go! We got some shit to talk about. Fuck these games, and fuck this mothafucka right here. LET'S GO!" Gary said glaring at me. He lightly pushed Darius out of the way. Darius bumped into me as I walked up to Gary.

"Gary, chill!" I said. The part of me that loved him really wanted to leave with him, but the drunken angry part of me wanted to show him how Detroit brothas get down with the hands, but I couldn't fight my baby…

"A'ight, dude, I tried to be nice about this shit," Darius said.

"Dee, chill!" I said turning in his direction pushing Gary back.

"Come on, I'll talk to you later, Gary. Chill, I'm not dealing with this madness tonight." My emotions once again were all over the map. Things seemed to be going in slow motion but were happening so fast.

"Jason, you bringing your ass home with me tonight. I'm done playing these fucking games," he said grabbing my arm. I felt like a rag doll at that point.

"Gary, I have already told you that I am not about to deal with this tonight! Get the hell off of me and move," I fired back elbowing him in the process. "And what the hell you mean, you tired of these games? You co-starred in porn with your ex, yet I'm the one accused of playing games?" I stated sarcastically shrugging my shoulders. Did he really just try that, I thought to myself.

Darius stepped back up attempting to separate the two of us. He pushed Gary off me into one of the tables that was next to us and knocked over some drinks. Andre walked over and grabbed Gary telling him to let it go. He was trying to pull him away from the area. I grabbed Darius who was visibly upset glaring at Gary. I turned to look at Gary. I could see the tension and anger in his face as well. I turned towards Darius who had both of his fists clenched ready to go to blows. He lunged forward as if to swing. I turned towards Gary in an effort to keep some distance between them. Gary ripped his way out of Andre's grasp and swung as Darius ducked. I tried to get out of the way as Darius swung a punch and hit Gary in the face. The next punch from Gary, which I hope was meant for Darius, hit me dead smack in the front of my face extremely hard.

I heard someone yell for security as my head hit one of the bar stools. My body crashed onto the floor. I was left in a daze as Michael and Shawn ran over to pick me up. I was pissed once I realized why I was on the dirty, grimy bar floor. I was trying to fight my way from Michael's grip as he and Shawn led me out of the club. I couldn't believe what had just happened. I was fuming. Everything at that point began to move so fast. I wanted to go back inside of the club to stomp the life out of Gary. I didn't see Darius anywhere and my head started pounding. I looked down at my shirt and noticed blood. I became livid at that point seeing red on my new shirt.

"I'm bleeding. Let me go, Michael! I'm bleeding! I'm about to kill this dude! I swear before God I'ma take your advice and kill him. Ol' bogus ass! Let me go!" I was so pissed I couldn't see straight. Michael would not   let me go no matter how hard I struggled. He tried his best to diffuse the time bomb I had become.

"You'll be fine once we get you to the house. I'ma need you to cool off, boy!" Michael demanded.

"No! Let me go, get the hell off me! This fool got some nerve to hit me in my damn face after he cheats on me with some salty Caribbean nigga with a face full of razor bumps…looking like he got a Nestle Crunch bar wrapped around his chin. Then gon' give me!…" I stopped myself before I let the cat out of the bag and tried to continue my rant without missing a beat. "I'm killing his whorish ass! Get the hell off me, Mike. I'm not gon' tell you again!" I said looking him directly in the eyes.

"Whoa, whoa, whoa! Training time out, Jason! He did what?" Michael said in a confused tone. "What the fuck you mean? He gave you what? This nigga playing with your health? And this is the first I'm hearing about it? I'm your brother, and you gon' keep some shit like this from me?!" he said further pinning me up against the wall like a painting.

19

"We got to get up out of here before the police get here. We can discuss that at the house Mike," Shawn pleaded. "Jason, where are your keys?"

"They're in my pocket! Now let me go! Why ya'll keep grabbin' on me? GET OFF OF ME!" I said looking up at the sky. I struggled to release myself from Michael's grasp.

"Jay, be quiet now. You are drunk and you need to calm down! I'm gonna let you go, but you need to calm down. Okay?" Michael said peering at me with a stern look on his face. "I can't believe you hiding shit from us now, especially me! THE FUCK! I'm tempted to let you go back in there so we can help Darius."

"Where is Darius?" I said ignoring Michael's rant. "In the club Jason!" Shawn said in a seemingly irritated voice.

"You gon' calm down?" Michael asked. He was trying to regain eye contact with me again.

"I need to be in there biting and fighting like Mike Tyson. Please let me go! Oh my God! Do you understand this fool hit me dude? Are you serious right now?!" I said as tears started welling up in my eyes.

"Yeah, and he also supposedly gave you something you ain't telling us about, but for now, I need you to chill. Are you gonna calm down?" Michael asked again.

"Yes! Damn!" I said as Michael loosened his grip. "And stop cursing, you don't even sound right doing

20

that," Michael instructed halfway laughing.

I unbuttoned my shirt and dabbed my lip. It was busted. I spit out a mouth full of blood. I wiped my face and saw Darius and Preston run around the corner towards us. "Dee, you alright? I asked.

"Yeah, we gotta go ya'll. These niggas gon' call the police in a minute. Your boy Javi got me up out of there," he said as I reached in my pocket to grab my keys.

"My damn jacket is in there," I cried. "You can buy another one sweetie," Preston informed. "Darius, can you drive him to the house safely please? He is drunk as hell."

"I got him. Come on, Jay. We gotta go. You alright?" Darius said walking up to me.

"Please don't grab on me right now!" I barked stepping away from him. I had been man handled more than enough for one evening.

I pushed the button to unlock the car. I gave him the keys and got in on the passenger side. Darius made sure I got in without touching me. He closed the door and ran over to the driver side to get in. He started the car, made a U-turn, and sped off down the street. I rolled the window down and spit out another mouth full of blood.

"Yo' baby boy, you alright? I'm sorry, Jay," he said sounding genuinely concerned for my well-being.

"My freakin' head is killing me right now," I said reclining the seat. "I can't believe he hit me," I said, finally putting my seatbelt on.

"He was trying to get at me, not you," Darius assured.

"That fool still hit me," I said dismissively. I rolled my eyes at Darius. "That's the last straw. Screw him. I'm going apartment hunting tomorrow. Busting my face all up. I don't believe this! I'm done with that fool!" I said looking out of the window.

"That might be the alcohol talking Jay."

"Whatever!" I said sitting up to look at my lip in the visor mirror. Darius pulled into the parking lot of a 7-Eleven. He left the car running and ran inside. When he returned, he handed me a bottle of water and some Tylenol. I moved the seatback upright. Darius grabbed the bottle, opened it, and handed it back to me. I took a large gulp, ripped open the packet of Tylenol and popped them into my mouth. I drank some more water until it started to sting my lip, which felt swollen.

Darius was silent as he looked at me. I rubbed the side of my head. I could feel the knot forming. He put the car in reverse and backed out. We made our way back to Shawn's house. He found a spot and parked. I opened the door and got out leaning up against the car. Darius walked over and helped me walk to the entrance.

"Dee, I don't feel good. My stomach is all queasy and junk."

"It's probably all the adrenaline that was flowing

through your body, not to mention, you did have a lot to drink. You'll be okay."

"Are you okay?" I asked. I turned my head in his direction.

"Yeah, baby boy. I'm cool. I just need to chill."

"I'm sorry you had to go through all that drama. I apol..."

"Shhhh. Jay, it's alright, okay. Which one of these is the key to the door?"

"The one with the blue tab." He opened the door, and we walked up to the apartment. We made it up to Shawn's apartment and I walked into the living room and plopped down on the floor next to the love seat. Michael and Shawn walked out of the kitchen.

"Jason, you okay?" Shawn asked.

"Do I look okay? I'm a product of domestic violence," I said.

"Oh, chile hush! You just got caught in the crossfire," Shawn said.

"Whatever. I want some ice for my lip. Oh my God. I don't feel good. Darius...can you...help me up?" I took a deep breath as he lifted me up. "I want to get in the tub and lay down."

"Shawn, I'm gonna help him out," Darius said.

"Cool. The bathroom is in my room all the way to the back," Shawn said.

"Jason, we will see you tomorrow okay. I got to get going. And we're discussing that little bombshell you almost dropped tonight, when you sober up. You gon' be alright?" Michael said.

"Yeah," I said waving my hand in the air dismissively.

I slowly walked to the back. Darius followed and helped me take off my clothes. I jumped in the shower and washed my face and body. I dried off and realized my bags were in the car. Shawn was lying on his bed. He told me that Darius was in the guest room and had brought my bag inside. I told him I would see him in the morning and walked to the spare room. Darius was lying across the bed. He looked up when I came in. I closed the door. "I feel a little better," I said, trying to muster up a plausible smile.

"You sure?"

"Yeah. Darius, I didn't mean to drag you into this, okay? I don't want you to get hurt. I'm going to talk to Gary tomorrow and sort this thing out. I need to handle our issues and come up with some type of resolve. You know?"

"Come here," he said. I walked over to the bed to lie down beside him. He held me and wrapped his arms around me.

"Jay, you don't have to apologize to me. I need to fall back and let you work this out. I realize I've been putting some unnecessary pressure on you. So I'm going to fall back and let you do what you need to do. Alright, baby?"

"Cool."

"Keep in mind that I'm here for you, a'ight?" He

said squeezing me tightly. He pulled me close to his body and my back molded to his physique.

"Cool," I said starting to relax.

"Yo', in hind sight, and I'm not justifying dude's behavior, but I will say this. I could see that man loves you. That punch wasn't meant for you, Jason. I can feel where he was coming from."

"I don't know. I guess. Did ya'll really throw down?" I asked looking over my shoulder.

"His boys broke things up. I regained my composure and got up out of there. Your boy Javi convinced security to chill, so they calmed everything down. He told me the owner of the club wasn't there tonight, but we all needed to dip out before someone made that call."

"Well, I'm glad ya'll are safe. Was Gary alright?" I asked truly wondering how bad the fight had gotten. I was genuinely concerned about him even after all was said and done.

"Yeah, I took it easy on your man," he laughed.

"Shut up!" I said nudging him in the ribs.

"Yo' your man's got a nice right hook though."

"You trying to be funny?" Reminding him of my injury.

"Oh shit! My bad," he laughed, "but, Jay, he hit me too."

"Yeah, he used to box when he was younger. He tried to teach me a few things after I told him I have never been in a real fight. I'm still mad he hit me though."

"Well, you'll be fine," he said kissing my ear gently.

"Yeah," I answered as he laughed.

"Damn, I ain't gon' ever tap that ass, huh?" he said thrusting his pelvis into me.

"Here you go! Don't start." I snickered.

"I'm just a man," he laughed.

"Yeah, I can feel that," I said trying to inch closer to him.

"You still love him?" he asked hesitantly.

"Don't ask questions you don't want to know the answer too," I warned in a low voice.

"I know you do. Just be careful, Jay," I didn't say anything. He continued to hold me as we faded into slumber.

I'm Doing Me...

One great thing that came about from this break-up was a different type of bond established between Darius and me. He was deployed again to Kuwait with sporadic trips to Iraq, and we were talking at least weekly. He reverted back to his old ways and all I could do was shake my head. Darius still wasn't sure if he wanted to mess with men or women. The boy always went back and forth, feeling the term bisexual doesn't describe his character. He claimed he was a full fledge gay before he was shipped off to Iraq the last time we talked. He was pulling my leg from what I gathered. I don't understand why he has an issue with it. His dad is on his side, so that right there to me should be the pen that signs the contract to live his life. But c'est la vie.

That night at the club he told me he was in town because his ex-girlfriend had gotten pregnant by him. I think the main issue was he was in love with this broad, but she was a challenge. He was on a mission to lock her down if you ask me. And from the pictures he'd shown me, I can't say I blamed him because the girl was gorgeous and could pass for Lauren London's twin. However, the caveat was her not wanting to keep the baby, but his plan was to set up shop for her because he didn't want her to have an abortion. He promised to make sure she was well taken care of so that he could be a great dad like his father. He didn't agree with abortion and forced her to carry to term, and the rest would be on him. I must say it was a very admirable thing he was doing. How he convinced his commander to ship him home for an R&R visit to handle that matter is beyond me. But if it's one gift the boy has, it's the gift of gab. We talked for hours in between sleeping and he expressed some of his deepest thoughts and fears about his current events. I wanted to tell him how much I truly liked him, but I didn't want to jeopardize the friendship and trust we had established. For now, I was simply envisioning him in my mind while enjoying our late night deployment conversations...

"Okay, these are not the pictures I was expecting you to send," I said with a slight laugh quickly answering the phone. It was late and I knew the only person calling from a sixteen-digit number was Darius. I was reviewing a couple of emails he'd sent the previous day.

"Yeah, they are. You said to send you some sexy pics. What's sexier than a big ol' hard chocolate penis?" Darius asked.

"Really, Darius?" I said laughing. "I mean, it is nice. But that is not what I wanted to see. Now you've ruined the surprise," I laughed. I continued clicking through the pictures attached to the email.

"Not really. To see it in person is yet another story. I want a picture of your face when that time comes," he said.

"Then your ol' nasty butt sent not one, but six different pics of your entire dick. Where were you when you took these? Glamour Shots for Ding-a-lings?" I smiled. I grabbed the remote and adjusted the volume on the television.

"Yeah right, nigga! I was in the bathroom getting busy with the digital camera."

"Well, I like them. But I want some of you in your uniform pants, shirtless, and some mug shots next time," I said shaking my head.

"I can hook that up. I took those 'cause I was horny as fuck," Darius replied.

"Wow. So anyway, did you get my care package?" I asked.

"I sure did. Thanks. I'm gonna eat me some Crunch N' Munch when I hang up with you. And how did you know I liked Raisinettes?"

"Because I know you, that's how. You always had an empty pack laying around your crib back in Lejeune," I smiled thinking about how messy his place would get at times. He kept a clean kitchen and bathroom, but the rest of the place would be a little disheveled.

"Awww, you been keeping tabs on your boy! That's what's up!" Darius beamed.

"Yeah, something like that. And ain't it like almost seven in the morning over there?" I asked.

"Almost eight. What time is it there?"

"Ten thirty-six, p.m. So how are you going to eat

31

Crunch N' Munch for breakfast? I asked."

"Because they're serving mystery meat and powdered eggs this morning. We still haven't got a supply shipment yet. I had some cereal, so I'll be straight," he said trying to convince me that junk food was a major food group.

"I remember those days," I laughed.

"Yeah, they're slackin' today. And my girl ain't there to hook me up today."

"What girl?" I asked.

"This chick that's feeling your boy. She tryna get this dick."

"Anyway! Did those CD's make it safely?" I asked, not wanting to hear about his latest female prey.

"Yeah. Good looking out with those, baby boy! I'm gonna upload them tomorrow."

"Cool. When are you going to be back stateside though?" I asked.

"In like a couple of months. Things are supposedly tentative right now. But I'm out of here as soon as I get the job done." Darius had been sent to Kuwait for a few months with a specialized medical team doing a case study on the stress fractures soldiers were experiencing from the boots issued for dessert use.

"You still enjoying your new found freedom?" he asked.

"Yup! I love my new crib. This is the first time I've really lived by myself, you know." I replied. "I finished the guest bedroom this past weekend."

"It's a whole new world when it's just you," he said.

"I know right. I love it. I can come and go as I please and don't have anyone to answer to." I said.

"I'm coming home to visit when I get back," Darius said.

"Cool, am I gonna see you?" I said lying back on the bed.

"You know not to ask crazy questions like that. Of course I'm gonna come see you."

"Cool. Just checking. I don't want to come in between you and that broad," I laughed.

"Never that. Bros over hoes!" he said jokingly.

"We'll see," I laughed.

"Alright, Jay, I gotta go. I got about a minute remaining on this card. So that's my cue to start my day. You going to bed?"

"I'm gonna stay up for a little while longer. I have some homework to finish," I replied.

"Cool, I miss you."

"I miss you too. Call me as soon as you can," I blushed.

"I will," Darius said.

"And let me know if you need anything else and email me. Cool?"

"No doubt. I'll holla at you later, baby boy."

"You have a good day. Bye," I said as the call disconnected.

Life was getting back to normal for me. It had

been almost a year since the break-up. It was as if I returned the hurt inflicted on me by Gary. I didn't want to do it, but the dynamic of what we had established totally changed. I felt I needed to break free. It hurt so bad that I now hate the taste of salt on my food because of the tears I've shed over our break-up. To further keep my mind occupied, I got my little pooch Batman. He was a black and brown Miniature Pinscher with pointy ears, which is why I named him Batman. The irony present in that decision clearly demonstrates that either way I would have ended up with a dog.

I put my phone on the charger and walked into the kitchen to pour myself a glass of juice. Batman trotted in behind me. I gave him a dog biscuit and we headed back to the bedroom. I lay on my bed and continued reading where I left off in my Sociology book. Batman curled up in his little doggie bed and started crunching on his treat.

I wasn't quite ready to date, but I was playing around with the idea and set up an online account for the sake of alleviating boredom. I was back in school and helping out my new friends Javier and Jerome with an open mic set called Poetic Expressions. I had recently purchased a pretty decent home on the city's north side using my VA loan with some encouragement and help from my Uncle Jesse. I even found a church. I wasn't attending as regularly as I knew I should, but at least I was still connected on some level. I was re-inventing Jason - not the wheel. I was finally doing me for a change.

In light of doing me, things were familiar yet different with Darius and me. I felt like if we were in the same city we would definitely be in each other's space all the time. His current unit was based out of Bethesda. He was trying to gain as much experience as possible with his physical therapy profession due to his recent residency towards his commission as a Naval Officer. I had to give it to him. He was on the up and up. Recently, he had been talking about going all the way and retiring from the Navy. I was in full support of this decision but not sure how that could affect us if we were to be together. He'd been dropping hints about me moving to D.C., but I have a life here in Chicago. This was home now, so I'm not sure what will become of us. I do have love for him and hadn't planned on blotting him out of the picture. Besides, he was about to be a father and I wasn't quite ready for a new owner.

I hadn't spoken to Gary for quite some time. Ours just wasn't a happy home anymore. I will always love him, but if I see him on the street it will be just a hello and goodbye. I was done. Michael told me he'd seen him posted up at this club downtown a couple weeks ago. He walked over and asked about me. Michael said it took everything within him not to hit him. I'm glad he kept his cool.

I had a little talk with Michael who was curious to

know what I was going to say that night at the club. I didn't feel comfortable telling him my situation, because I wasn't fully able to deal with the fact that my ex compromised my health like his did. He offered support and told me that if I needed to talk in my own time, he'd be a listening ear. He told me that he was facing some issues with his current lab test results. He was optimistic that things would be fine, yet he was still concerned about them. Not only that, he was dealing with his mother going in and out of the hospital lately dealing with diabetic issues and high blood pressure, so the last thing I wanted to do was to add to his stress. I am your typical Aquarius; I can depend on myself, I don't need anybody else, when it comes to my emotional stuff.

I was always concerned about Michael when it came to his health. We would talk about the whole HIV thing from a general standpoint or when it was the basis of a joke. He never let the virus slow him down and he lived his life as if he didn't have it. He would always inform me that I needed to use condoms so that I wouldn't become a statistic. "Men like this thing called life offers no prizes nor guarantees," he always said. Michael was like a big brother to me and I felt like I had let him down. He teased me saying that I let Gary get away with murder. In hindsight, that was closer to the truth than anything I had told him.

I guess the natural thing to do with an ex is to lash

out, or have this unhealthy dose of hatred for them. But that's a waste of energy if you ask me. Now don't get me wrong, I was pissed, and sad, and enraged, and hurt. I was every emotion imaginable, but you have to count your losses, decide what you will and won't tolerate, and carry on with the duty known as life. The best way to get back at an ex is to get over them. As long as they feel you still thirst for them, they will always sniff around your door to play on your vulnerabilities. I didn't want to end up having Gary play on my emotions like that. It was bad enough I was sort of letting Darius do that to me. You've got to realize that life goes on. Go out and find someone who is adult enough to be with you for you, with minimal baggage as possible. Today's music will lead you to believe that cheating is cool, expected, and forgivable. To me, not so much. Either fix what you have or move on. Contrary to popular belief, cheating is not the new monogamy.

Gary talked a good game trying to convince me to stay, but the reigning question in my head was, what for? He, in so many words, had given me a free pass to cheat unbeknownst to me two days prior to me viewing his amateur porno tape. He kept asking me all these weird questions of if I ever thought about being with other guys, and if our relationship was enough for me. I could sense something was off, but equated it to him getting older and I being younger than he. Do I miss him? Yes. Do I love him? Yes. How will the so called new me act when I see him again? I honestly don't know. What is he going through lately? I wonder if he is having these same thoughts.

Gary's Hurting Too...

Jason, I miss you, baby. I miss my man. Every day that lil' nigga gone drives me up the fuckin' wall. I can't get him out of my head. I fucked up royally and I couldn't even right my wrong. Jason threw me for a loop when he said he couldn't stay with me and he left. I can say he seriously tried to give it a chance, but I think he felt like I was tainted. He told me he felt like I didn't belong to him anymore. This could be true. A part of me had still held onto my ex-boyfriend Desjardin because there was no closure. I could have sworn I was over that fool. My dick got me in trouble. I guess I can't even blame it all on my dick like that.

I know I would have wanted to bust some heads and shit if Jason stepped out on me like I did. So I can't say that I blame him for washing his hands of the situation. Fuck! I miss my baby. I'm sayin', this man used to be there for me. He cooked for me; I especially miss those creamy cheesy grits he'd make me for breakfast on Saturday mornings. He kept the house in order, dealt with my stubbornness and temper, helped me to be a better me, had a sick head game, and that ass was molded to my dick because I was his first. I might not ever get that kind of love again. It's rare to meet someone you can completely be yourself around while being intimate at the same time. He could see through all of my bullshit and allowed me to recapture some of the innocence this world can strip away from you. He made me remember what it used to be like when things were new and exciting. Now that I've tampered with his seal, he'll never be the same. For that, I hope he can forgive me. I thought we'd always have each other even if the world crumbled around us. Jason is the real deal. He's a mate who compliments me rather than compliments me. He defines what it means to have a partner, so how the hell did I fuck that up?

It's been eight months and let's see, what's today? Wednesday? Yeah, eight months and seventeen days and I'm still hanging on. I want my baby back before the New Year of '05 hits. Somehow my brain won't let me comprehend the fact that he's gone. I've tried checking for other kats, and freaked with a couple of em', but substitution is not as satisfying as authenticity. I wonder if Jason is thinking about me or missing me. I kind of think he's over my black ass. And as much as I keep telling myself that, I'm not ready to wrap my brain around this shit. I gotta snap out of this somehow. Eight months' worth of mourning is crazy. One of the hardest parts next to facing him about it was telling Moms about our break-up. She was devastated. I guess because she could see that I was truly happy and honestly, she loved him just as much as I did. I can say that Jason was and will always be the love of my life. Damn, eight months' man, and I'm still trippin.

I'm sitting here lying in my bed half dressed with

the T.V. on mute. I'm listening to Kem's, "I Can't Stop Loving You," through my headphones, knowing I got to get up in a few short hours to go to work. I got Jason on my mind like a wave cap. Not only is it just one of those nights, it's getting close to the time when we first met. I remember spotting him laughing and smiling with his friends. I thought to myself how much I wanted to be the reason he was smiling. He has such a sparkle. When I was face to face with him and made him laugh for the first time, that smile warmed my soul. I got my wish. I could not get over how beautiful this man was and how bright his smile was. It helped me to let my guard down. Hmph, the combination of his deep brown eyes and that smile sent this tingle through me. Like he had flipped a switch, and shed light on a place within me that everyone else neglected to see.

To think of someone touching him and him giving them the same type of affection he once gave me angers me. When my boy Andre alerted me that he was up in the club shaking his ass for some lame, I immediately got dressed and stormed out the house needing to see the shit for myself. When I locked eyes with the fool who had his dick pressed up against Jason's ass, I lost it. I didn't give a fuck at that moment even though my rational mind was telling me, fighting wasn't the best way to address the situation.

But when you love hard, being rational sometimes

isn't an option. I ended up hitting my babes in the face by accident. Real speak; I'm not even sure if it was on purpose, or if he just got in the way, or what the fuck. But deep down, I didn't mean to hit him. I can't forgive myself for that one. When Jason and I first met, I told him that he would be the next Mr. Larrieux. His reply was if the stars aligned in my favor. I knew he was the one in that moment. All I know is I'm not giving up the fight, that's my heart, my all, my rib, my family.

Back on the island, my great granddaddy and I were really close. I was his favorite probably because I was the only grandkid who was patient with him. He was one of the wisest people I've ever had the chance to know. I remember him saying to me that some things are rare and hard to come by. He was deep into astrology and gave me my first telescope. The night he gave it to me, he said in his heavy Caribbean accent, "Boy, dere are tings in dis world dat you will only get to enjoy and experience for a brief moment. But dose tings will leave a lastin' impression upon ya. You gonna see what I'm talkin' bout ta'nite, but undah'stan what I'm sayin' to ya latah on in dis life," he winked his eye at me and smiled brushing my chin with his fist.

It was 1986; I think I was thirteen going on fourteen and my young curious brain was trying to make sense of what the old man was saying to me. He hyped up the return of Haley's Comet and made a picnic on the beach for just the two of us. He told me that when he was around my age in 1910, that his Paw Paw sat him down on the very beach we had set up camp to witness the same event he was going to share with me. He was excited explaining that he had waited 76 years for this day to come. We were skipping rocks off of the ocean that afternoon and looking at the stars later that evening. Out of nowhere, the most beautiful burst of light exploded in the sky. It was the big comet known as Haley returning in all of its glory. My granddaddy smiled like it was an old friend passing by. I followed suit by waving and jumping up and down excited that he had chosen me out of all the people on the island to share that moment with.

A guy like Jason only comes around once in a blue moon, and if you're lucky you can relish in his presence for a little while. I pray he will return and spend some more time with me like Haley's Comet did for my granddaddy. But this time I pray it's for keeps. Damn, I regret what the fuck I did. I miss you, Jason, wherever you are. Fuck, I miss my man.

Put A Read on It...

I was going to miss helping Preston with his papers for class. It was another moment the judies had all been waiting for. Preston had finally graduated from the Art Institute of Chicago. He was almost done with his internship with Niemen Marcus and was ready to pursue a career in fashion. He wasn't sure what he wanted to do, but his creativity and fashion sense were unparalleled. He was indeed a wet dream of a label whore within our group, but he wasn't boastful about it like many of the kids are when it comes to designer threads. He kept us all in the know on what was in and what was out. And always rocked the latest.

We all decided to do a nice dinner for him and hit the club afterwards to celebrate Preston's accomplishment. It had been a few weeks since we had all been together. For the crew, this was unusual, but we were all so busy lately. I rushed home to walk and feed Batman and to change clothes after the graduation ceremony because I came to the event right after work. I also needed to pick up the lasagna I made and the cake we all purchased for him. I then headed over to Shawn's house because the nights' events were going to start there. Shawn had invited a few of our mutual friends to hang out later. I called Shawn once I arrived to tell him to preheat the oven and to send someone down to help me bring the stuff into the house.

"Bitch, what the fuck is up, honey?" Shawn said smiling. He started sashaying down the walkway towards the car chanting the house mix, "Walk for Me."

"You are so stupid. How are you?" I laughed taking a moment to observe the animated behavior of my friend.

"Chile, I'm feeling my cocktail," he said giving me a quick firm hug.

"I see. Here grab the cake. I put it in the trunk," I said hitting the key fob. "Hopefully, it's still intact. I tried to take it easy on the turns."

"Yeah, I know how you drive. You did bring the lasagna right? Cause, bitch, the girls are hungry," he rubbed his stomach as he made his way to the back of the car.

"Lasagna? I thought ya'll asked me to make my famous chit'lins and cream cheese casserole?" I said smiling.

"Ewww! Jason, don't play. If you didn't bring no lasagna, me and the judies are gonna go in hag!" Shawn said lifting the hatch.

"I know, chile. It's right here," I said closing the door. "I brought some wine too."

"Alright, whore! Giving grown and sexy tea, I'ma have to dig out them wine glasses bitch," he said chuckling.

"You know it!" I said as we headed up the

48

walkway to his building.

"Chile, oh, um, I know how you feel about Lyzell, but he's here for the graduation party hag! So play nice," he said with a cheesy I'm sorry type of smile.

Lyzell was an old friend of the group whom I could only take in small doses. He and I had a misunderstanding back when we were all stationed in Camp Lejuene, North Carolina. I had to drop off some specimens at the lab over at the main hospital and overheard his loud mouth behind talking to one of his queeny friends about how he and Michael messed around, but he didn't let him get the goods because Mike was sick and going around spreading AIDS like the rest of the pretty boy sissies in America - his words not mine. When he realized that I heard him, he tried to play it off like it was a big joke by hugging on me. I disowned him as a friend after all was said and done vowing only to be cordial when around him because everyone else was still friends with him. I never told Michael what was said because I don't like to perpetuate drama, and I was still new to the group. So this was going to be my break in case of emergency read if need be. I did, however, give him a heads up to be careful who he lays with and tells his business too. Even to this day, I think I am the only one other than that queen who knows Mike's tea.

"Okay and? Why you telling me that?" I said in a carefree tone.

"Well, chile, I don't want any weird vibes in the air

49

between you two thunder cats. He's only staying for dinner. And dessert. And the club tonight. And possibly brunch if you go," he chuckled before letting out a burp.

"Thunder cats though?" I laughed.

"Yes, Cheetara! You know how you two queens go at it like, it's MY ball of yarn! No, it's MY ball of yarn! MEOW! MEOW! HISSSS! HISSSS!" he said bursting into laughter.

"Shawn, I will be cordial," I said laughing his comment off. "I'm just glad I put on my big boy draws this afternoon," I said taking a deep breath and counting to three. I smiled and continued. "Did you give that hoe this same speech?" I said trying to alleviate any preconceived notions he had about my feelings.

"Sure. Alright, I just want you to keep it cute for cuteness sake. You sure you'll be cool?" he asked again as we made our way up the walkway.

"Shawn, if you don't go on upstairs. Yes, I'll be cool." Admittedly, I was slightly irritated at the idea of him being in town, but he was in the picture before me, so I would have to swallow my pride on this one. Shawn stopped me before we made it to the door.

"Okay, and Andre is here too," he said really fast. "Come on, whore, let's pooch! KEE KEE!"

"Dang, Shawn! Next, you'll be telling me that my grandma and her prayer circle will be making a cameo," I rolled my eyes so hard I almost fell asleep.

50

He pushed me through the door as I continued. "I'm bound to run into one of Gary's friends sooner or later. And the fact that you are dating his homeboy increases those chances. It's cool. Now let's go eat these chit'lins," I said laughing. I was mentally preparing to get my nerves worked.

"Jason, I swear if you brought chitterlings up in through my house it's gonna be a knock down drag out, bitch. I will REEEAAAD you for pure points, bitch!"

"Well, I suggest you get your boxing gloves out and put your glasses on hag! I thought that was a delicacy in the South," I teased. We made our way through his apartment door and Michael and Lyzell ambushed me.

"Hey, bitch. Give me this so I can put it in the oven. OOOOH this is gonna be so good," Michael said mocking Paula Deen. He snatched the pan and bag of wine out of my hands and hurried into the kitchen.

"Hi to you too, Michael!" I yelled. I was trying to formulate a nice greeting for Lyzell in my head.

"Bitch, what's tea? Was that that nasty ass lasagna I heard so much about?" Lyzell asked laughing not missing a beat.

"Lyzell! How are you trick?" I asked. I took my jacket off and hugged him with as much sincerity as I could muster up. He was already trying it. This was not going to be easy for me.

"I'm good. What about you? You doing all right? I

heard about the break-up," he said putting his arm around me. "You two were the gay version of Will and Jada! You know I don't know personally, that's just what I heard, honey!" He said ushering me into the room as if we were the best of friends. I quickly sharpened my blade. And by blade I mean my tongue. I see I was going to have to eventually cut this messy queen down tonight.

"Boy, that was so long ago. I'm so good. I'm working and doing grown up stuff, you know me?" I expressed with cavalier sentiment.

"Well, actually, I barely know you, girl! We gotta play catch up. Get some teas exchanged, girl!" Lyzell said as we walked into the living room. I closed my eyes. Each time he called me girl, it grated on my inner soul like nails on a freaking chalkboard. He was doing it to be catty. "Well, I have the perfect man for you. You just gotta move to San Diego," Lyzell cackled. "You know, I'm California dreamin', right girl?"

"Yeah, I heard. But you know I don't do the pigmentally challenged. I'm allergic to white boys," I said trying to ignore his attempt at breaking me down.

"Don't knock it till you try it, Jason. Them white boys will take care of you. But I was talking about this black guy. He is about your height, brown skinned, bald head, pretty teeth, with a very nice build." He placed extra emphasis on the part concerning the guys build. "Jason, this boy got a body out of this world. Solid muscle! It's like hugging a tree trunk, bitch, he so hard. Damn!" He said sipping his cocktail. He started doing a shimmy.

"Okay, I'll book my flight out tomorrow," I joked.

"You better jump on him before someone else does. He's an intellectual type. I know you like them kind of boys. Chile, we had a conversation at work one day about the importance of Barack Obama running for president and the upcoming election, and I was so bored I almost choked on my yawn. I don't like to talk about politics honey."

"That's too bad, Lyzell," I said feigning a smile.

"I'm dating this JAG officer. He's a Lieutenant Commander," he stated proudly. A JAG (Judge Adjutant General) officer in the military is one who works in the legal field. "I'm gonna be an officer's, wife honey. Yes, ma'am, Pam! I'm doing new things this quarter, girl," In my head I was thinking your loud country behind ain't hardly going to be nobody's officer nothing. I wanted to scream: QUEEN, PLEASE HUSH THE ENTIRE HELL UP!

But I promised to be the adult in this situation. "A white guy?" I asked.

"Of course. White boys are in season. Ya'll sleeping," he said pointing at me. "Last year, it was Asians. I had to upgrade from trade pieces like Beyoncé said in her song honey. You heard it, right?"

"Yes, I'm familiar with that track," I said resting

my jaw in the palm of my hand as we sat down. "Oh, so you're a candidate for affirmative action relationships," I said laughing.

"Okay! I don't discriminate. Just call me an equal opportunist, girl," Lyzell said. He was oblivious to the read I just administered. He slapped me a high five. I had only been here five minutes and this boy has referred to me as girl five times. That's one girl per minute! I took a deep breath and told myself to remain patient.

"You look good, sir. Your dreads are coming along really nicely?" I said, thinking a compliment might soothe his inner tiger. Really, his inner "pussycat."

"Yeah, chile, I been growing them for about three years now," he said running his fingers through them. "Bitch, the dates love to pull on them, girl. My officer piece said they feel like Cheetos. I had to read him for filth about that, and he took the girls to the jewelers the next day honey. You like my bracelet, girl?" he said dangling this gaudy yet expensive looking trinket in my face.

"Oh, that's nice Lyzell, so this is what assimilation; I mean California dreamin' gets you?" I was avoiding eye contact with him as I ran my index finger over the top of it. "Okay, nice. If you like it, I love it," I stated with a pasted smile on my face.

"Yes, girl, not as bad as I thought it was going to be. I got my hook-ups in all the right places, so it's been pretty nice so far."

"When did you get in town?"

"Early Thursday morning. My hubby didn't want me to leave," Lyzell gushed. "You know he proposed before I left, girl. I told him maybe, honey, but I'll wear the ring on the trip to think it over. See how it matches the bracelet?"

"Cool, well I got you on drinks tonight to celebrate," I said trying not to roll my eyes. I was thinking how unfair life was. This queen had the ring. It was the first time that I agreed with Bush's decision to ban same sex marriage...just to be spiteful. "Okay, be careful with them promises," he warned.

"I know right!" I laughed. I looked up at the ceiling for a couple of seconds and said a quick prayer. Lord, please give me strength. This is a test that I'm trying to pass.

"Cause you know I can drink," Lyzell said laughing.

"I know, I forgot. Lyzell, you look good. I see you got your high school shape back." Truthfully, he had slimmed down since the last time I saw him. His dreads framed his face quite well, and the San Diego sun had definitely done his skin well. I remember how we would joke with him telling him if he'd been left in the womb a little while longer he would have been a girl. His face was masculine, but oddly enough he had subtle soft features.

"I know, thank you. Jason, the Cali life will do that to you. The only thing you have to do is exercise, party, and work. My hubby wants me to watch my carb intake. But I'm gonna eat something un-Godly while I'm here. Fuck a diet," he chuckled. "Bitch, he got me a Bally's membership. I thought I was gonna die that first month."

"Well, don't kill my pockets tonight. I gotta buy Preston a couple of rounds also," I said looking to segue out of this conversation. Apparently, the rest of those hags wanted me in here squirming to free myself from the grip Lyzell had on me.

"He a light weight, so I'll pick up his slack," Lyzell said.

"Speaking of which, where is Preston with his ol' gay self?" I asked.

"That bitch is in the back taking a shower and designing his outfit for the evening. You know how that queen is?" Lyzell laughed. He picked up his cocktail and took a sip and crossed his legs. Andre came into the living room with Michael and Shawn.

"How long does that thing need to cook? I'm starving," Michael said sitting down.

"It should be about 30 minutes. You put the oven on 350, right?" I asked.

"Shawn said you said 450. I knew that didn't sound right," Michael laughed.

"No, 350, Shawn is drunk," I said, as he ran back into the kitchen.

"What's going on, Jason, how you been man?" Andre asked walking over to greet and hug me. I stood up and embraced him.

"I'm good. How have you been?" I said.

"Pretty cool. Just keeping up with your boy over there. He running me ragged," he smiled pointing at Shawn.

"Really, Andre? I see how it is?" Shawn said folding his arms.

"You know I'm playing baby," he said kissing Shawn on the lips.

"So what have you been up to, Andre?" I asked.

"Man, to tell you the truth, just work. It's been crazy at my office. Congratulations on your new crib Jason. It's a pretty good time to buy," Andre said.

"Thank you. Yeah, I see the prices are starting to drop because the market is slowing. I should have waited a tad longer, but I'm happy with my purchase," I said.

"Yeah, man, something major is about to happen with this economy. I can feel it," he said sounding sure about his statement.

"Well, let's hope it doesn't get too bad," Michael said.

"Alright guys, seriously, I have to run. I'm gonna go and let you and your friends do what ya'll do best," he said pulling Shawn up off the couch. "Save me some lasagna, boo. Ya'll have fun tonight."

"Alright, Andre, see you later," I said, followed by Michael and Lyzell. Shawn walked Andre outside. They kissed and hugged. Shawn walked back inside and locked the door behind him.

"I hope I didn't scare him off?" I said.

"Chile no!" He said dismissively. "He knew we weren't gonna do nothing but cackle like school girls," Shawn said. "There's not enough testosterone in here for him tonight."

"Speak for yourself," Michael said.

"Girrrrl..." Shawn said rolling his eyes.

"Chile, I'm glad he left. Now you can catch me up on the lowdown with you and that bastard you used to date," Lyzell said. He kicked off his designer loafers and crossed his legs again. "And he better be paying child support leaving you to take care of that dog all by yourself," Lyzell said as I laughed.

"I'm sure Shawn filled you in about that," I said glaring at Shawn. He shrugged his shoulders and waved. "It was too general and vague, bitch. I want the muthafuckin' TEA!" Lyzell said snapping. He took a sip of his cocktail and flipped his hair like a white girl.

"Well, there really isn't too much more tea to pour," I said smiling at Michael.

"All I know is that fool approached me in the club a few weeks ago all up in my ear asking about this, bitch," Michael said pointing at me. "I wanted to push his fro back to the 70's, swear to God," Michael said pounding his fist into his hand.

"Michael ignored the man and kept it moving thank God," I said.

"Did you ever find the bitch he cheated with?"

Lyzell asked.

"Hell naw! I'm not looking for him either," I said.

"Hmph! Ain't he a good one?" Shawn said looking over at Michael.

"Bitch, you peed, cause see I'm a classy girl now days!" He made one of his grand dramatic pauses for effect. His lips were puckered at this point. All that was missing was a drum roll to quere his next statement. "But two or three days ago, I'd still be doing muthafuckin' cartwheels up and down the hallway on a bitch face for messing with my man. And my man's face would get some   fierce   cunty cartwheels   for   dropping   dick in another bitch draws without MY expressed written consent!" Lyzell said as Shawn screeched, YEEES! I couldn't help but laugh a little.

"Right, cause I would..." Michael said as I interrupted.

"We know what you would do." I chuckled. "Long as you know boo! Because I'm so over sorry!" Michael boasted. He and Lyzell slapped each other a high five.

"Have you run into Gary?" Lyzell asked sipping his cocktail. He batted his eyes and sat his drink down on a coaster.

"Surprisingly, no I haven't. It's been a minute. Not that I'm looking for him either," I said looking at my phone.

"Hmm. There's some tea there," Shawn said smiling and rubbing my back.

"Did you catch that too? Let me see your phone," Michael chimed in. He got up from his seat and snatched my phone from me.

"Boy stop! I am not checking for Gary like that," I said.

"Your call and text log will tell me differently," Michael smiled going through my phone.

"You're a mess," I said smiling and rolling my eyes.

"Jason, you back peddled once, so you might do it again," Shawn said.

"I know right! You should have held out for that ring girl," Lyzell said holding his hand with the ring and bracelet up in the air. I decided to take the high road on this one. I shook my head at his blatant disregard to my feelings.

"You know what? I tell you hag's too much of my business. That's tea," I laughed.

"Who else you gonna tell if you don't tell us?" Shawn said.

"I'm gonna find a new group of friends," I said smiling.

"Chile, good luck with these new girls," Shawn said laughing.

"I'm serious! I can erase ya'll numbers and start over. Delete is a three step process," I said pointing at each of them.

"But your friendship contract ain't! It's till death. We ain't Gary, bitch. You can try to leave if you want to," Michael said with a stern look. We all burst into laughter.

"You know what? I'm truly convinced that you are crazy. Yes, I'm convinced," I said shaking my head laughing.

"As long as you know," Michael said gripping my arm. "I love you to death."

"I know right. Let me go check on my food. We're eating at the table Shawn?" I asked. We all filed into the kitchen.

"Yeah, we can. That'll be more family like," Shawn answered. I opened the oven to peek at my pasta creation. "It needs about 10 more minutes. I can put that bread in with it," I said.

"I tossed a salad for ya'll earlier," Michael said smiling.

"I bet you did, ol' nasty ass!" Lyzell said looking at him. He bent over slowly to adjust his sock. Michael smiled shaking his head. He was pouring more Vodka and Apple sour mix into his glass. I rolled my eyes and grabbed a baking sheet from the cabinet and placed the garlic bread onto it. Preston walked into the kitchen and hugged me.

"Thanks for making dinner, Jason. This is so sweet of you," Preston said.

"Hey, divot! It's the least I could do," I turned around and hugged him tightly. "How you feeling, graduate?" I was so proud of his accomplishment.

"Oh I am so glad it's over, sweetie. I didn't want to believe it until they called my name and handed me that diploma," Preston said grabbing a bottle of water.

"Chile, that's how I felt when I graduated hygiene school. It's a totally different feeling than graduating high school. After high school, you feel like oh my God, what's next? It really feels like the end; you know what I'm saying?" I said.

"Yeah, I know right because now I know exactly what I'm going to do. I didn't feel like that after high school," Preston said.

"Are your parents still here?" Michael asked.

"No, they got back on the road. They had to get back," Preston said.

"It's good they came," I said.

"Chile, my no good boyfriend claims he couldn't find the graduation hall. I am so over his late ass. Ugh! Since you didn't show up to my graduation, I'm cutting you off. Someone please hand me a Valium," Preston said looking at his phone and swooning.

"Boy, you so silly. He text that to you or some tea?" I asked laughing at his exaggerated gesture.

"Here sip this cocktail, honey," Lyzell said handing him a martini glass.

"Yes, chile that'll work," he said holding his glass up in the air. "Look at what his late ass wrote," he said showing us each the message.

"Where do you find these guys, Preston?" I said. "I'll give you some graduation dick later. Wow!" I said reading the text aloud.

"Chile, not tonight! Do you know who I be?" Preston said looking at me placing his hand on his hip.

"A classy brotha' who deserves better than that," I said putting the bread in the oven. I closed the oven and turned to slap Preston a high five.

"Sweetie, that's why I'm doing this right here," Preston said showing me that he was deleting the contact out of his phone as we both laughed.

"What club house we going too?" Lyzell asked.

"The Generator! It's on and poppin' again," I replied.

"And please tell me ya'll are going to pride this year?" Lyzell asked.

"Well, I'm not going this year. I have an event to help out with that weekend," I said.

"What event is going to cause you to miss Ms. Atlanta Pride, chile?" Lyzell asked. He said sounding disappointed. I wanted to say because you're going to be there, that's why hag!

"Boy, the reason this ho ain't going is because it's going to remind him of Gary?" Michael chimed in.

"No, it is not HAG!" I laughed. "I'm helping host a Poetry Slam that weekend to promote gay youth bullying awareness," I said.

"So he says?" Shawn said.

"Are you going Shawn?" Lyzell asked.

"My family reunion is that weekend, so I'll be in Virginia," Shawn answered.

"So it's just gonna be me and bighead?" Lyzell

63

asked referring to Michael.

"Yeah, I guess. I think these ho's gon' drive right?" I said.

"Yup, because I'm going too," Preston said.

"Lyzell, why are you so concerned about   black pride when you're dating some white man?" I said laughing. I removed the food from the oven, and placed the pans on the stove.

"I can still mingle with my people. I can adapt to all environments. Open up Jason, you should be able to do that being the progressive one in the group girl," Lyzell snapped.

"I can. I just don't see myself with a white guy," I said shaking my head. "And can you stop calling me girl? Please and thank you," I said trying to sound as pleasant as possible. I was about ready to grab my keys and leave. Lyzell sucked his teeth and smiled as if to say whatever bitch.

"Be nice, boo!" Michael said winking at me.

"Who's hungry?" I asked. I rolled my eyes at Michael negating his last comment.

"Oooh I hate you, Jason!" Michael laughed putting his arm around me.

"Here's a plate," I said smiling. We all fixed a plate and sat at the table. Shawn blessed the food and we continued talking about random things going on in each other's lives.

"Jason, where you living now?" Lyzell asked. "Over on North Pulaski in Albany Park.   How long you gonna be here?" I said.

"Until next Thursday. I'm going to go home to Virginia for a couple days and then meet these two girls in Atlanta," Lyzell said.

"Cool. I kind of wish I could go with ya'll," I said.

"You can whore!" Shawn said.

"I have an obligation to the community, Shawn. I can't go now," I said winking at him.

"Chile, bye. You can go, whore!" Shawn laughed. "Speaking of obligations, did you tell Michael about your online date?" Shawn continued laughing.

"What date? You know we got to start screening these dudes you be picking," Michael said.

"Shawn you're so messy. And Michael I'm grown," I said smiling. I took a bite of food.

"Word to the wise. If you're dating a top, then his credit card should go on top of the bill. Gay dating 101," Lyzell said as he and Preston slapped one another a high five.

"I suppose, I only set up a profile," I said to Michael, shaking my head ignoring Lyzell's ignorance.

"But the tea is, Jason, you aren't going to really find nothing, but nymphos, porn stars, druggies, and AIDS online anyway," Michael said.

"Oh my God I know! I got a message from this white dude that said: 'Love to eat ass. Would you like a good ass eatin?' If I didn't kee kee," I said.

"YES WOULD YOU LIKE A GOOD ASS EATIN!" Shawn screeched, as he and Lyzell burst into laughter.

"I know you replied yes, right?"

"OKAY!" I said slapping Shawn high five. "Getting them cakes ate is wonderful," I laughed. "But seriously, the Internet is a mess. This crap is all new to me though. I mean, coming out of a relationship and starting from ground zero is a trip. Not to mention scary. I can't tell the real from the fake. Or in this case the horny from the un-horny."

"Well, only go online if you want anonymous sex. You can meet someone just being out and about. That isn't a hard thing to do. You ain't ugly, so that's half your battle right there," Michael said.

"Cause, chile, if you were ugly you might need to use the party line," Lyzell said.

"Okay! They'll fool you on the party line with a deep voice and fierce description. You get all the way over to the Southside to meet what you think is trade, and a muthafuckin' 6'8", big dick drag-queen opens the door bitch," Shawn said as we laughed.

"I remember you telling us that. What was that things name?" Preston laughed.

"HA! Maurice! More like Marlene. I just knew I was about to get it in. You hear me?" Shawn said slapping Preston high five.

"Speaking of online hook-ups, Michael, do you have a list of bootys alphabetized and scheduled for your trip?" Lyzell asked.

"Bitch, he doesn't need to go online to meet a freak in the ATL," Preston chimed in.

"Thank you, Preston," Michael winked.

"I wonder if you can have a successful relationship living there," I said pondering my own question.

"Baby, I don't see why not. I mean it's like any other city right. You can cheat anywhere. But it takes a fierce bitch like myself to get that good gay wedding band," Lyzell said waving his tacky ring and bracelet in the air for like the 13th time this evening. I rolled my eyes at him.

"I don't think I could do it. It's too concentrated with boys. All that booty running rampant! Mmmm, mixed with my sex drive. Nope, my hometown would not be a good move for me," Michael said.

"I think if you put your mind to it and really focus on the one you're with, you can make ATL work. Your old running buddy Jesse does just fine down there," Shawn said.

"Jesse is a whore bag, Shawn. I've witnessed that," Michael said.

"Hmm. Pot, kettle, black," I said getting up to walk into the kitchen.

"You opened yourself up for that one sweetie," Preston laughed.

"I hate you Jason!" Michael yelled as he and everyone laughed.

"Dessert anyone?" I asked looking around the table.

Nakedism...

Life was finally putting the whipped cream and cherry on top of my dessert. It was the day of my big promotion to Lieutenant. I had finally made the cut. All of my hard work had paid off. Everyone close and important to me was there including Jason who I had selected to pin me. Damn! My baby looked good. He had on a nice tailored grey suit, a starched light blue shirt, with a nice navy blue and yellow striped tie. Now Jason doesn't wear suits too often, but when he does mothers hide your daughters!

My commissioner read off the citation and promotion letter. I stood there basking in the moment. It was time to get pinned. They called for Jason to come up to do the honors. He was smiling ear to ear as he made his way up on the stage. My fire chief handed him the insignia. Jason walked over to me and waited as the members of my crew rendered a hand salute. I returned the salute and turned to face Jason. His smile slowly faded as his eyes welled up with tears. I studied his face as he mouthed a few words. I couldn't understand what he said initially. It looked as if he was telling me he was proud of me. But the silence was set aflame as his words became audible. "I can't do this!" He said crying. Those words cut like a knife as Jason gracefully walked up to me and placed the gentlest kiss on my cheek.

He gripped my hand and transferred the insignia

to mine. I heard the audience gasp and whisper as he turned away from me. The sound of his dress shoes rapidly tapping the wooden floor echoed off the walls of the building with thunderous percussion. He left me standing there as he ran out of the Auditorium. I looked down at what he'd pressed into my palm. My heart skipped a beat once I realized what it was. There in my hand was the ring I gave him.

The next thing I remember was a fire alarm going off and the sprinkler system dousing everyone with water. This turned out to be my alarm clock going off and me being drenched in my own sweat -a cold sweat indeed. Startled, I jumped up, and reached over to turn the clock off. It was 6:15. I sat up and placed my head in my hands. I was engulfed by the darkness of my bedroom. I rubbed my head and proceeded to the bathroom to take a shower. I needed to start my day.

The only place I can escape my thoughts of Jason are when I'm at work or at the gym. Any idle time I have forces my mind to a place of him and me. It's crazy and becoming stronger the closer it gets to our anniversary and the date we met.

I caught up with my boy Andre at a bar over on Clark and Sheffield after work. We were going to shoot some pool. I was hoping he could talk some sense into me and help me clear my head. I got there first and ordered a couple of Heinekens. I took a long swig of mine just as Andre walked up and popped a squat.

"My dawg! What up, what up?" Andre asked as I slid the brew his way.

"Shiiid, I can't call it. You got next," I said as we dapped each other up.

"Oh fa'sho, I got you," Andre said.

"You been alright, how's Shawn?" I asked.

"Shit's been good man. I can't complain. I'm happy. Only big thing going on is the market is beginning to slow, so if you trying to get a new crib, then holler at me man. I got loans to grant and property to move," Andre said.

"Man, I know. I gotta get my head back in the game, Dre. Fuck!" I mused rubbing my face.

"Don't tell me you still hurtin' over Jason?" he said turning his body in my direction.

"Yeah," I said taking a swig of beer. I pursed my lips hating to admit it.

"Yo', pretty lady, let me get two mo' of these," Andre said holding up the bottle. The bartender came back with the drinks. Dre placed ten bucks on the bar. "Come on, dawg, let's get this game started and let me holla at you, cause this is getting ridiculous, bruh."

"I know it is, Dre, I'm trying. I'm thinking about this boy more than ever dude," I said depositing a dollar into the pool table to release the balls. I started to rack them.

"Gary, you really need to snap out of it. It's been what 6 months?"

"Eight and a half. And I'm having fucking nightmares about what happened and shit. What the fuck is wrong with me?"

"Why is it taking you so long to get over Jason?

You bounced right back after Desjardin," Andre said.

"Dre, it was totally different with Jason. I was in a different place or a different type of love with that nigga. Ain't no other dude had me the way he got me. Then it's getting close to the time we met and shit," I said.

"What the fuck did Jason do to you? This nigga really got a hold on you," Andre smiled. He was chalking a pool stick.

"I sound like a bitch, don't I?" I laughed.

"You said it -not me," he said gesturing towards me. "But, dude, I been hurt before too, but this is some deep shit. It's like you're in mourning. The nigga ain't die on you," Andre said sipping his beer.

"It feels like it," I said lining the Q-ball up to break.

"Damn, that ass must be fuckin' incredible. Because that's the only reason I can see you trippin' like this," Andre laughed.

"Ey nigga, watch yo' mouth!" I said smiling.

"Shiiid, he ain't yours no more. But real talk, Gary. Do you think Jason is thinking about you? Do you think he's losing sleep? Do you think he's drowning his sorrows at the bottom of a liquor bottle?" Andre asked.

"Probably not. But who knows?" I said shrugging my shoulders. I prepared to take my next shot.

"All I'm saying is, you gon' let this shit consume you man, and you gon' miss out on the bigger picture. Not to mention another blessing. You fucked up. Deal with it and keep it pushing. I think the both of you have had time to get over the loss of what ya'll had. And there is always going to be a place for you in his heart and vice versa, but you got to get on with life, Gary. I saw your boy the other week and I can assure you that he ain't really pressed," Andre said.

"Where you see him at?" I asked. I stopped my shot and looked up at him.

"He was over at Shawn's celebrating their homeboy's graduation," Andre said.

"How did he look?"

"He looked good. Damned good I might add, but more importantly he looked how you should be looking. Over this bullshit! He looked as if he is moving on with his life. You feel me?" Andre stated matter of factly.

"Yeah, you're right man. I need to get it together," I said taking a sip of beer.

"That's right! Shake it off, baby," Andre said walking over and patting my shoulder. "You gon' be alright. You need to venture back out there and start dating again. Better yet start fucking again. When was the last time you smashed some ass?" he said taking a chance at the corner pocket.

73

"Damn, nigga I can't recall. Ain't that some shit. I'm thinking about a month ago. Shit, I don't know," I said.

"Yeah, you need to get you some ass. Quick! Or at least get your dick sucked. Shit! Stop thinking about what you've lost and think about what you've gained man. You didn't think you could find someone after Desjardin and look at what happened. You did. So take what you've learned from that and roll with it. It may take you a little bit more time to get over it, but the point is not to stay down man. I can see this ain't gonna be an overnight thing. Get yo' ass back up and start walking again. You feel me?" Andre instructed.

"I feel you, man. Thanks for the pep talk, Dre," I smiled and nodded my head.

"Anytime. You my dude. You've been there for me, so I always gotta return the favor. Now let's finish this game so you can go and find you a new playmate. Damn a month or two. Your balls blue as Wrigley Field Stadium, ain't they?" Andre laughed.

"I'm gon' fuck you up, Dre. That shit ain't funny," I laughed.

"I'm right huh?"

"I do need to get some," I laughed.

"My dawg. That's what I'm talking about! That's the first step to nakedism. Admitting you need some ass."

I left the bar feeling a little better. Of course I wasn't completely over it. But like Dre said, this wasn't going to be an overnight thing. There were still pieces of the mess I'd made left to clean up. I knew I had to get over this thing though. Dre was right, and I knew Jason. He's either hot or cold. And when he's through with something, that's it, he's through. So I know he ain't thinking about my black ass. If he was, he'd be here. I headed home and jumped in the shower. I dried off, walked into my bedroom, and popped a flick into the DVD player. I pressed play and grabbed my phone. I was thumbing through my contacts to see if any of the names would spark my interest for some late night company. I stopped at Jason's number. I stared at it and debated on deleting it. The name changed to D.J. as the ring tone sounded. I thought to myself, 'Why the fuck is he of all people calling me?'

"What?" I answered.

"Gary?" he said.

"Yeah, what do you want? Why you calling me?" I asked.

"I just wanted to talk to you. Please don't hang up. Do you have a minute?" Desjardin asked. His accent had lightened over the years.

"I'm listening," I said taking a deep breath. I was determined to remain calm.

"Are you alone?" he asked.

"If you don't tell me what's up dude, I'm hanging up," I said.

"Well, I'll take that as a yes. I um... want to talk to

you in person if it's cool. Can I come over?" he asked.

"Sure, why not?" I said. "At this point I have nothing left to lose." Maybe I can get some sympathy ass in the process I thought.

"Okay. Where am I coming too?" he asked. "Hang up and I'll text you the address. Hurry up, I gotta be to work early tomorrow," I said hanging up the phone. I texted the address to Desjardin, turned the DVD player off, and switched the cable on. I walked over to my dresser and slid a pair of basketball shorts on and pulled a wife beater over my body. I lay back on the bed and flipped through the channels. About 30 minutes later, I heard the doorbell ring. I walked down the hallway and looked through the peephole. It was Desjardin. I opened the door and leaned up against the beam.

"What's up, sexy?" he smiled.

"Why am I letting your ass up in here?" I responded.

"I wanted to talk and set the record straight. I just want to clear the air. I'm talking with a therapist about all my issues and she recommended I right my wrongs," he said.

"A therapist?" I chuckled.

"Can I come in? Please?" he asked. He put a puppy dog look on his face. I stepped aside, and half-heartedly motioned for him to come in. I noticed he was sagging his pants a little below the waist. He had on a pair of low cut briefs. Them cakes weren't

Jason's, but tonight, if it goes down, they'll do. Box that booty and leave is the theme for tonight.

"Have a seat," I said. I slouched down on the love seat as he sat on the couch. I wasn't sure what to expect from this nigga. It was a lot dealing with him just being here.

"First, let me apologize for what I did. I should have been more...I mean I didn't have to resort to that level. I know I messed up your little happy home," he said motioning his hand in the air like there was a fly bothering him. There wasn't an ounce of sincerity in his apology.

"Desjardin, I should beat your muthafuckin' ass for what you did, but I'm at just as much fault for bustin' up my home as you are. So now what? Why you even here, man? You knew what it was," I said.

"I know, Gary, but you hurt me, and I had to get back at you in my own selfish way," Desjardin said.

"What the fuck you mean I hurt you?" I asked sitting up.

"Gary, you stepped out on me that night. You hurt me first," he said.

"Desjardin, you starting to piss me off talking in riddles. We met up, we smashed, I felt guilty cause all these feelings I had for you came from a place I can't recall, and I left. You walked out on me way before that. So what the fuck is you thinking?" I said trying not to raise my voice.

"Gary, you cheated on me," he said. He was trying

to create a few crocodile tears to pull on my heartstrings. Wrong answer dude!

"Nigga! I did what?" I asked with a   screwed face.

"I saw you with her." Suddenly, he stopped acting. "You were kissing your ex fiancée the night I left. It was the day I bought you the rug for your living room. I saw you Gary! I saw you and her kissing and God knows what else! I saw you! I can't compete with a woman. If that's what you wanted, then you could have told me. Then I find..." he said as I interrupted him.

"Hold up! You saw me kissing Camille? When and what are you talking about?" I said thinking back trying to recall the event he accused me of. I scrunched my face up in confusion.

"It was when you were living in Roger's Park. You two were out on the patio. I drove back up to your place because I forgot my badge for work that night. You reached over and kissed her. It was more than a peck on the cheek. You guys were feverously groping and kissing. I saw you! You're going to lie to me about that?" He paused. I thought back to the events of that particular day in question. "I didn't stick around I drove off. That's why I left that night," Desjardin continued.

"Oh hell naw. I remember! I know exactly what day you're talking about, Desjardin. I should fuck yo' shit up! FUCK! Rather than confront me about it, you…" I clenched my fists and took a deep breath before proceeding. I was glaring at him. "This is what fucking happened. She called me the night before because she wanted to give me back the ring and necklace I gave to her when we were together. She didn't want to keep it and she didn't think it would be right to pawn the shit. We talked, exchanged some laughs, and last minute apologies. You witnessed an innocent kiss goodbye. End of story!" I said.

"So you didn't fuck her?" he asked with a puzzled look on his face. "NO! Why the fuck didn't you just talk to me about this shit!?!? You jumped to conclusions, harbored these feelings, and fucked up the best thing that's ever happened to me. Desjardin, real speak, we had our time. Fuck me for not being able to place all the blame on you," I said pounding my chest. My heart was racing. "Got-damn it! It was bad enough you jumped to conclusions, but you send a video of us fucking to my house as a birthday gift. That's some sick fucked up shit. Why the fuck would you do that?" I said slamming my fist down on the coffee table. He jumped as the vase I had in the center of the table tipped over and crashed to the floor.

"I wanted your little trophy boyfriend to know that you're not so perfect. I wanted to get back at you and you needed to be taught a lesson. So when your cousin Hannah told me about the party on my last trip back to the islands I felt like this could be my opportunity to get even. I just had to see this little boy you replaced me with," he said with a hint of jealousy. I raised my hand for him to stop.

"Desjardin, it would be in your best interest to raise the fuck up out of my house before I lose everything else I have," I said. I was breathing heavily. My heart was beating hard enough to power my truck.

"Gary, don't be mad. I'm just being honest," he said. Rather than him obeying my last order, he reached into his pocket and pulled out a tube of cherry Chap Stick and applied some to his lips before continuing, "Just say you forgive me, so I can let my therapist know I'm making progress. I have to get you to sign this letter of forgiveness," he said holding up a folder with a pen attached to it. He then closed his eyes. "In the immortal words of my girl Pebbles, 'we can make it work if you take away the hurt from the heart.' That's beautiful, right?" I couldn't believe how this fool was carrying on. Was he crazy?

"I'm not going to tell you again. You'd better go before I make eye contact with you or I swear knuckles and black will be the last two things you see," I said. He got up slowly and made his way out. He opened the door and turned to look at me. I got up and rushed towards the door.

"I'll just sign it for you. I remember your handwriting anyway. Gary, by the way, how did your little "doctor's visit" go?" he said with a fucked up smirk on his face. He was making one final attempt to get a serious rise out of me.

"LEAVE!" I said charging towards him. I pushed his ass down to the ground so hard I heard his back smack the pavement with gusto. I slammed the door, locked it, and made my way to the kitchen. I slung the refrigerator door open and grabbed a Heineken. I twisted the cap and pounded half the drink down before slinging the door closed. The coupons and magnets slid off as I flung the bottle top on the floor and walked back to my bedroom. Unbelievable!

The Freakin' Puerto Rican...

I was rushing home for like the tenth time this week. I had to walk and feed the dog, take a shower, get dressed, and make it to the south side all in an hour. I was excited about assisting with the Poetry Slam coming up this weekend. Javi and I were going to map out the layout for the event at a building we selected in Roger's Park. It was a pretty nice building, and we were satisfied that we had secured the location in time.

I completed my errands and made it by the skin of my teeth. God was looking out because I was able to find a parking spot directly across the street from the center. I grabbed my binder and rushed inside. One of the staff members greeted me as I walked in and escorted me over to the area where we'd be hosting the event. She pointed out Javi who was sitting on the stage writing in his notebook bobbing his head. He had set up his iPod and a set of speakers. Javi was so cute. He was wearing a pair of black Forces, a black New York fitted cap, a slim fitted military jacket, and a pair of ripped jeans. He smiled and slid off the stage when he noticed I made it. I had to admit that my crush on him had grown since I started helping out with the poetry sets, but my heart was more cautious now a-days than my brain when it came to dudes.

"What's going on, papito?" Javi asked. He embraced me with the warmest hug I've had in a while.

"Not much, Javi. I'm sorry I'm late. You know how traffic is around this time. How long have you been here?" I asked as we walked back over to the stage.

"Not long, I walked over."

"Oh yeah. I forgot you live around the corner and junk," I said.

"How was your day?" He asked.

"I had a busy yet uneventful day. I had a full patient load, so the day went by pretty quickly. Thanks for asking. Did you have a good one?" I said.

"I was off today, so I'm pretty relaxed," he laughed.

"Yeah, I see, you look good," I smiled nervously flirting.

"I see something better though," he smiled winking at me.

"Mmm hmm. Tell me something," I said.

"What is there to tell?"

"What you know 'bout that De La Soul?" I asked pointing to the iPod.

"Awww now you've insulted me. You dare question my hip hop awareness?" he said folding his arms. "These are my dawgs!" He cleared his throat and recited a rhyme: 'I'm shakin' hands with many devils in the industry, believe the Genesis life fill with stills mean that I'm def, so like the autographs you sign until the Break-a-dawn, break-a-dawn. Break-a-dawn, break-a- dawn.' What you know?" he said folding his arms in a b-boy pose. "Cause I'm a hip-hop nerd, papi!"

"Oh alright, I got you," I said clearing my throat. "'I don't cuff mics, I ruff mic's up, ruff and rugged, yet the girls still love it. Still an old five-o came to my mic check, telling me that I left lacerations around my mics neck. Domestically disputed and you just might get the undisputed underdog serving ya'll threat.'" I said reciting a verse from 'The Grind Date' album.

"That's my track right there. 'And what we have is much more than they can see!'" He sang. "Not too many people know about that one."

"I know. I like Lupe's version of that song. Please tell me you've heard his mix tape?" I asked.

"Yeah, I got that on a disc somewhere. I know it. Check you out, pa. Let me find out you ain't about the mainstream," he said smiling.

"That's another reason I write. I like the joints that be saying something. You know?" I said nodding my head. We smiled at one another during an interim of silence.

"Cool. Well let's get started. I'm gonna have to quiz you later," he said giving the back of my neck a squeeze. It had been a long time since someone's touch sent that type of warm bone shaking sensation through my body. It was something my body craved again. My soul wasted no time feasting on its presence. Gary used to do that same thing to me.

"Come on with it," I said flashing a smile shaking

off the memory of my ex.

"Okay, this is tight. We got the stage of course, so we can put the Deejay up there. Shareef is going to spin for us that night. You remember him right?" he asked.

"Yeah, I do. Thick dude with all the wild hair?" I asked.

"Yeah that's him. He deejays at Spin for hip hop night. He's hot right now. I think he'll elevate the intermissions."

"Yeah, I liked him at the last event. I was thinking that we could close off this door and have people file in from the back. They could pay outside the back door. That should keep the foot traffic on lock," I said.

"That sounds cool with me. One thing I was thinking was that maybe we should have a section for the artists for time sake. I mean this is a big room. What you think?" He asked.

"I see what you mean. But you know not everybody is going to be feeling that because they are going to want to sit with their friends and junk. But that is something to think about. On second thought though, if we do that, we can pin numbers on the slam contestants and that will make the judging easier. Yeah, let's do that," I said.

"Cool, so we got that taken care of. So we'll have them seated like over here on the right side, and they'll enter over here up the stage. And I like your other idea about the judging. That way we don't have to pay anyone," Javi said.

"Oh about giving boards to a few audience members?" I asked. "Yeah, I mean I'm thinking about time. You know?" Javi said.

"I feel you. So I will bring five slates and some markers for the audience and one of us can tally the scores. We need to do that at all the slam events. We'll just pick five random people."

"Yeah, I'm feeling that. That should work," Javi chuckled as he jotted some notes down in a notebook. "Ya' boys coming?"

"Unfortunately no. Mike and Preston are going to black pride in Atlanta, and Shawn has a family reunion to go too," I said with slight disappointment in my voice.

"Man that's too bad, they're gonna miss out," he said shaking his head.

"I know. It is what it is. They keep pressing me to go Atlanta with them," I said.

"Aww now don't flake on me, papi. That wouldn't look as good as you do," he said looking up from his notes.

"No, I ain't gonna do that. I'll be here. I'm excited about this. I worked hard on this. This is my first slam," I said blushing from the latter part of his statement.

"You nervous?" Javi said smiling at me. He walked over to the stage and he packed up his iPod and speakers.

"Not yet," I said grinning from ear to ear, hoping he was talking about the slam.

"Good, it'll be fine," he said winking at me. "Say, did you eat yet?" he asked.

"No. I didn't have time," I took a glance at my watch.

"Ditto, I haven't eaten either. Check this out, let me take you to this Puerto Rican restaurant on the West side. You'll love the food kid. I'm telling you. Hook you up a nice plate of arroz con gandules y pepper steak, huh, what do you say?" he asked nodding his head yes.

"Dinner with you?" I said smiling. I was trying to think of an excuse to say no, but nothing came to mind quickly enough.

"Yeah, sort of an um...informal date," he smiled.

"An informal date?" I inquired looking at him suspiciously.

"Yeah, until I build up the nerve to ask you on a real date. This is practice," he laughed. "So don't hold anything against me." He bit his bottom lip and shook his head. He was looking at me like he wanted to attack me. He licked his full cherry red lips. The wetness left behind from his tongue shined in the light illuminating from the light fixture above our heads. His eyes were full of a desire that seemed to want to escape and disregard candor.

"It's something wrong with you, Javi," I said laughing and breaking the eye contact.

"I know right; I can't believe I said that. So what's up? Will you join me for dinner Jason?" he extended his hand out in the direction of the door.

"Of course I will," I said as we walked towards the office of the center. I was going to need to be careful with this one, I thought to myself, with his charming tail.

Javi and I went back to his apartment so that he could pick up his car. I was going to follow him to the restaurant and make my way home after we ate. We had light conversation and I think there was a nervous energy being emitted from the two of us. Deep down inside, we both liked one another, but I was avoiding saying it out loud. I wasn't sure what I wanted from a guy at this point, and he was an awesome new possibility.

After dinner, I made the drive home. I was greeted with a warm welcome from Batman who had the run of the house. I was in such a hurry that I didn't put him in the kennel. The last time I left him out, he teepee's the place with a roll of toilet tissue. It was crazy because somehow it didn't break. He had a perfect flow of tissue coming from the bathroom trailing down the hallway, into the living room, through the kitchen, and finally ending at the front door. I couldn't do anything but laugh. He was good this time. No new surprises.

I took him for another walk and then readied myself for bed. I had a pretty long day and just wanted to relax. I was still excited about the Poetry Slam coming up. I really wanted everything to go off perfectly. Hearing some of the artists at these events inspired me to perfect my own craft and push the envelope in terms of my writing. It took me a long time to really let others hear my prose. To truly know me is to read my words.

My thoughts shifted to Javi. I thought about how much fun he was to be around. I also thought about our informal date tonight. It was pretty chill. There wasn't any weirdness -just a lot of playful flirting. The sexual attraction and tension had always been there, but who knows where things will go. I wouldn't mind getting it in with him either, but at this point in time I was kind of scared of sex thanks to my ex.

Chock it up to my paranoia getting the best of me. Maybe I was saving something for Darius. I could not wait for him to bring his butt home. I was trying to have fun being single, but maybe we could be more. The tea is: Am I ready for more? I laughed to myself for over analyzing everything. That's part of the Aquarius mind set though. I cut the lights off and got comfortable in bed. My dick was hard from thoughts of both Javi and Darius. I had a hot threesome with the two of them in my mind as I jerked myself into a deep comfortable dream.

Life's Scars...

This was the first weekend that I didn't have anything pressing to do. I wanted to sleep in but still managed to wake up early. So I cleaned up my place and finally hung the curtains in the guest room. I then put together a bookcase for the room I was using as an office. I was still full of energy, and since, I was sweaty I decided to go for a run. It was pretty nice outside. I took Batman along with me so that he could get some exercise. He was all tuckered out once we rounded the corner back to the house. I opened the front door and went and grabbed a dish from which he could drink from. Batman followed me back outside and patiently waited for me to fill the dish with water. I began a set of stretches.

During the middle of my set, a guy on a motorcycle pulled up into the driveway. He was wearing a wife beater, jeans, and a pair of Timberland boots. His helmet matched the green and black sport bike he was riding. He parked the bike and took his helmet off. It was Javi looking sexy as hell. His hair was all curly and tapered fresh from the barber shop. This boy was perfection wrapped up in well-designed package. To say he was cute would be disrespectful. He was freakin' gorgeous! I was wishing I had a mirror, so that I could have made sure I was looking cute enough for him in my workout gear. I smiled as he walked up towards me.

"Boricua! What's up? I didn't know you rode a bike?" I said. I smiled and removed my ear buds, thinking to myself again how phone he was.

"I know. That's turning you on, huh?" he said flashing me his pearly whites. I started to answer his question with a yes, but decided against that. I'm sure he gets told how good-looking he is all the time. I'm not going to sweat him like that I said to myself.

"Don't flatter yourself," I said punching him on the shoulder. I pushed pause on my iPod. Control your erection, Jason, I thought to myself, you have on basketball shorts, bruh.

"I just got it a couple months ago. I haven't really made time to ride it. So why don't you come enjoy one of the last days of summer with me. Let's go for a ride."

"You're not going to lay the bike down are you?" I asked. I was curious to know how long he had been riding. I remember riding on my uncle's Honda Goldwing from time to time when I was a little boy.

"Oh course, you know I always got you Jason, don't even trip!" he smiled.

"Alright, I guess I can do that," I smiled.

"What were you working out or something?" Javi asked. He was squinting his eyes from of the sun.

"Yeah, I just finished some calisthenics and a light jog. I had the dog with me, so I couldn't really max out," I said sitting down to do a butterfly stretch.

"Who, with killer right here?" he said sitting on

the porch steps. He started messing with the dog making kissy faces.

"I guess he likes you, because he'll usually bark and shy away from people," I smiled enjoying the sight of his interaction with Batman. Batman looked to be falling for Javi's charm, and I couldn't blame him.

"That's what's up? That's because I'm good peoples," he said as Batman sniffed and licked his hand. "Ain't that right killer? What's his name?" he said focusing his attention on me.

"Batman," I said as the dog ran down to investigate what I was doing. He was standing on his hind legs trying to lick my face. I gave him a few back rubs as his wet nose tapped my chin.

"What you doing with that little bitty dog? You need a guard dog."

"I can't deal with anything bigger than him," I said rubbing his belly.

"Little gay dog. He's cute though," Javi said with a slight chuckle.

"Ain't he? He's a good judge of character also," I said looking up at Javi. I winked my left eye and smiled.

"Oh yeah? Well, I like the company you keep, Batman," he said winking back and smiling at me.

"So where you taking me?" I said trying to resist his powers.

"You gotta get ready first," Javi chuckled.

"I know, but it would be nice to know where we're going," I said.

"You don't always have to be in control of your destiny, but since you asked, I wanted to go chill with you by the lake. Is that alright?" Javi asked.

"How you know I didn't have other plans?" I said standing up.

"Two reasons. Either you would have told me when I asked the first time, or you wouldn't be here at home," he said standing up as well. We entered the house and walked to the kitchen.

"Maybe you're right. It's beautiful outside," I said stating the obvious.

"I know, so you need to get ready so we can enjoy it," Javi said.

"Alrighty, already, chill," I said handing Batman a treat. He took it and ran under the dining room table.

"I came all this way and don't get a hug or nothin'?" he said with his arms outstretched.

"I'm all sweaty," I smiled.

"I'm all sweaty!" he said mimicking me. "I'm not tripping on your sweat. I can triple that," he said grabbing and squeezing me.

"Really?" I said hugging him back.

"Alright, go now. Smelly boy! ! Vamanos!" he smiled.

"Shut up! You know how to work the T.V. and fix you something to drink if you want. And don't be down here man handling my dog," I demanded before running to my room to shower and get ready.

We left the house and cruised through Boys-town as we made our way to Lakeshore Drive. I held on to Javi's waist and enjoyed the ride. I don't think there is anything sexier than a dude as phyne as Javier on a motor cycle, rocking a set of gloves, wife beater, jeans, and Timbs. His tan arms glistened in the sun as we made our way to Sheridan Beach on the Drive. I had on a grey tank top and some ripped jeans and some grey and white high top Force's. We parked the bike and took a casual stroll down the strip.

We found a shady area near the water to just sit and talk. Javi leaned up against the wall by where we were sitting. We weren't really saying much at this point, but he broke the silence by asking me the strangest question I think anyone has asked me. Strange as it was it was thought provoking.

"Jason, have you ever been afraid of yourself?" "Hmm. That's a good question," I thought about it for a second and extended my arm out to him with my palm facing the sky. I gently rubbed my wrist revealing a scar I will never forget.

"What happened here?" he stroked my scar with his index finger. It tickled slightly as I thought of how I would express this personal injury to him. I took a deep breath and touched his finger.

"Well, I remember when I first started grappling with the fact that I was a gay," I smiled shaking my head. "Um, I had to be about 11 going on 12. Well, I

97

had always heard my mom and dad talk down about being gay and junk. They made it very clear about how despicable they felt it was." I paused and thought about some of the comments they would make, especially my mom when she would watch talk shows that had gay guests," I paused again and looked out towards the lake.

"You alright, papi?" Javi asked, rubbing my shoulders helping me to relax.

"Yeah, yeah, yeah, I've never told anyone what I'm about to tell you," I smiled. I looked into his eyes. I hadn't even shared this information with Gary. I guess it never came up.

"So what happened?" he asked ready to listen intently.

"Well, like so many other gay youth, you think about either running away or taking your own life. I decided on the latter choice. So, I planned to slice my wrist open and bleed out. I had the knife picked out and everything?" I said shaking my head. It felt strange to say that out loud. The thought of it sent a cold chill up my spine. I was so young thinking that I was a mistake. If my family was rejecting me, then what would the world do? It's amazing how deep a kid's mind can go. Thank God that I was able to receive the two most important lessons I've ever learned in church. God is love and He loves me. And God doesn't make mistakes, but man does.

"Word? At 11?" he asked.

"Yes. I had a plan mapped out," I said grabbing a twig that tumbled its way over to us in the warm summer breeze. I started to manipulate it with my fingers. "My dad was taking us to a company picnic the day I was going to do it, and my mom was going to be working that night. I was going to do it when my dad and sister were sleep. It's crazy because I didn't even feel bad about it. I don't know what I was thinking Javi. I wasn't myself," I chuckled. "Well, at the picnic I was playing with my sister and some other kids and I ran up on the slide. I must have been in a hurry to slide down or something." I looked up at Javi then back down at the twig I was playing with. "I didn't let go of the handle in time, and one of the other kids was running up the other side to catch me. I think we were playing tag or something." I smiled. "So, like, as I was sliding down, my wrist got caught up on an old rusty screw. And that is how I got this scar." I said.

"So you obviously changed your mind," he said rubbing my arm.

"Yeah. I did! Quickly, that mess hurt like hell!" I said laughing. I threw the twig into the air and fixed my eyes on his. "So I was like I cannot go through that for real. It made me realize that my life was worth more than that bit of pain. It's crazy because I haven't thought about taking my life again. God saved me that day." I paused and looked over at a couple of kids on skateboards doing tricks. One of them fell and the other ran back to check on him and helped him up. "I mean we are all here for a purpose. Some for good and some for bad for God's will. So yeah, I am scared of myself because I have the ability to make choices. I'm scared of myself because I was in a mind set to take my own life. And over what, someone else's hatred towards me."

"Whoa, I wasn't expecting that. That was heavy," he smiled.

"Yeah I know right?" I laughed. I studied his face for a second and then looked down at my wrist. "So this scar is a reminder to never take life for granted. Live your life for you. It also lets me know that God is still with me," I said then looked up at him and smiled.

"Well thank God for this scar," he said.

He grabbed my arm and locked eyes with me. He brought my wrist up slowly to his lips never letting his eyes leave mine. He kissed my scar and smiled. He placed my hand on his cheek and pulled me close to him. The two of our faces were so close I could feel his minty breath tickle my lip as he exhaled. He then closed his eyes and I followed suit letting him take the lead.

Our lips gently pressed together sending a tingling sensation through my body that was very familiar to me. We started off slowly at first and then a ferocious wave of passion engulfed the two of us like the water from the lake nipping at the shore. We began to kiss deeper and deeper, our tongues interlocking with precision. Those pretty red lips were as soft as they looked. The crazy part about it was the way he kissed me reminded me of Gary so much that I envisioned it was him there instead of Javi. I didn't know how to interpret that.

"Damn, you taste mad good kid!" he smiled closing his eyes letting out a grunt.

"Thank you," I blushed. I wiped some of the moisture away from my bottom lip, avoiding eye contact with him this time. It reminded me of how Gary and I used to kiss with blind regard to our surroundings. It was so hot and a free love type of feeling as the breeze washed over and through us as it made its escape through the limited space between our bodies. No restrictions, no inhibitions, no reservations, but no Gary this time. I felt guilty oddly enough.

"I…um, yo', my bad Jason. I didn't mean…" he said, as I shook my head no.

"Javi, it's cool," I smiled. I knew what he was going to say.

"Word, you okay, papi?" he asked.

"It's cool," I said slowly nodding my head.

We eventually wrapped up our outing and Javi took me home so that he could get ready for his sister's birthday party. We both told each other we had a great time and agreed to meet up again soon. I watched him ride down the street wishing he were Gary, before heading into the house. I walked down the hall to my office to turn on the computer. I then walked to the bathroom and opened the door to let the dog out. He bounced around me and started barking letting me know that he needed to go outside.

Instead of walking him, I decided to just let run him around out front. I sat on the porch and called my mom. Surprisingly, I didn't get voicemail. Usually, she was at work or had her phone hidden deep within her purse. She picked up on the second ring.

"Mama, what up? What's going on?" I asked. I was still in a state of euphoric bliss.

"Nothing, where you at?" she voiced gruffly.

"I'm at home watching this silly dog roll around in the grass. What you up too?" I smiled.

"Nothing," she said sighing. She had Heather Headley playing rather loudly in the background. It wasn't blaring, so I knew she wasn't directly near the speaker, but it was very loud.

"Mama, why are you listening to that ol' sad depressing song with the volume way up?" I laughed. She never listened to any dismal music, and to have it up that loud, was different for her.

"I just am," she said in a huff.

"Ma, what's wrong?" I asked. I could hear something very different in her voice.

"Your daddy and I are getting a divorce. There I said it. It's out in the open. It's over and done. I'm through with his ass," she said, letting out an audible exhale.

"Ma, stop playing," I said resting my elbows on my knees. Batman ran up on the porch and stretched out next to my thigh. I began to rub his back not knowing how to process her news.

"Do I sound like I'm playing? We split up," she said.

"Are you okay?" I asked realizing how stupid and immature that question may have sounded to her.

"What do you think?" she snapped. Her response startled me. She paused to collect her thoughts and continued. "I'm sorry. I'm just under a lot of stress right now."

"Where is he?" I asked. I waved to my neighbor who was waving hello to me. I put a quick smile on my face and redirected my attention towards my mom.

"Probably with the ho he sleeping with. Your guess is as good as mine. If you talk to him tell him the locks have been changed."

"He cheated? With whom?" I asked. I looked up to my dad despite our differences, but this put me back in the head space I was trying to steer clear of.

"Some girl from the church out here? She sings on the choir? Supposed to be good Christian folk and running behind a married man. This ain't the first time this shit has happened. This really pisses me off."

"I know, Mama. I know."

"You know what?" she asked.

"I can only imagine how you must feel." I said

103

choosing my words carefully. I did not want to step out of line. I had my suspicions about his first situation. My dad is very social, charming, and an incorrigible flirt with the ladies at times. A part of me is always leery of this type of behavior when I meet a guy. It can get you caught up which is why I'm in the situation I'm in I guess.

"Oh. Well, she can have him. I'm done," she said.

"Well, Mama. I wish it was something I could do. I don't know what to say. Will you be all right?" I asked. Batman started licking my hand as I rubbed his muzzle.

"I'm just pissed right now. I'm hurting. And you and Jasmine need to remember that's still your daddy. No matter what we're going through. I don't want ya'll taking sides. This is our fight. Okay?"

"Yes Ma. I can't believe this. Ya'll just gon' give up 24 years of marriage?" I asked in disbelief.

"It was based on a lie anyway Jason," she barked.

"Ma, what you mean?" I said confused.

"Nothing. Forget I said that." She sucked her teeth. The song in the background started over.

"Well, Ma, I'm going to come out there. I want to see you and know you are okay."

"You can come on," she sighed.

"Okay. I will let you know after I make some arrangements."

"Well, let me get off this phone boy," she said. "Okay, Mama, you're going to be fine.   You aren't like most women. You'll get through this," I said trying my best to show my support.

"Maybe," she said.

"Have you talked to Jasmine? You told her yet," I wondered how she was handling the news.

"No... I haven't," she said taking a deep breath.

"You want me to tell her?" I asked hesitantly. I really didn't want too, so I was hoping she would say no.

"Yeah. I'll call you later."

"Okay, Ma. I love you."

"I love you too," she said in a low tone. She doesn't normally tell me she loves me at the end of a phone conversation. My mom is weird like that. She is a hard woman and rarely shows any emotion. This was yet one more thing to make this beautiful woman unable to soften. I think that's where I get it from because I am notorious for putting walls up. I can most certainly sympathize with her. I can relate to the pain she is going through. I had to muster up all the courage and strength I had to get over Gary and move on. Now, Gary and my dad's face were synonymous with one another's.

Are relationships meant to last? I mean if my parents could go through life together for 24 years. And ball it up like a piece of paper and toss it out the window, then what hope do you leave your children of having happiness with that one person. What made my pops cheat? What does his side of the story look

105

like? And what is the truth? What's left? It makes me question so many things about love, happiness, and monogamy.

I wasn't sure how I was going to tell Jasmine. I also wasn't sure how I was going to approach my dad. I was pissed at him for what happened and I intended to get down to the bottom of it. I wanted to clear my head and process the event my parents would soon embark upon. Divorce. It's so final, yet inchoate due to the proceedings and the aftermath. I thought about Gary and I. Then back to my parents. What's up with the breakdown of relationships? What happened? I stood up with that same numb feeling I had when I found out Gary cheated. I went inside the house.

"Batman, come on boy. I got some calls to make. Come on batty boy," I said patting my leg and opening the front door. I didn't think that feeling would come back so soon. Shake it off Jason. Shake it the hell off, I thought to myself, visualizing images of my own break-up.

Mom's Mirror...

I was chilling going over some notes at my desk for this promotion board I'd been preparing for. I was truly on a mission to get this promotion and elevate my career. I gotta make the board this time. I'd been neglecting my baby, but Jason understands that this is going to provide more income for us. Not that we're struggling or nothing, but more disposable income is always a good thang. He wants us to save up for a trip to the UK, which I'm down for. My baby got so many dreams. And whatever I can do to see them come true, I'll do.

My thoughts were shifting to him and how I could make him even happier. I guess I was really in a daze because there he was staring and smiling at me when I snapped out of my daydream. He was holding a container of food. He laughed at my embarrassment.

"So this is how my hard earned tax dollars are being spent?" Jason laughed.

"Be quiet, Jay," I laughed. "What'chu doing up here baby?" I asked.

"Since I'm such a good man, I brought you some lunch. I noticed that you left your food on the counter at home," he said sitting the plate on my desk.

"Aww my baby! Always looking out for your man," I said as he sat down. I opened the container and walked it over to the microwave. I punched in two minutes and closed the door.

"So are you studying or daydreaming because that didn't look like studying to me," Jason smiled looking at my book.

"I just got a little sidetracked. That's all," I said sitting back down in the chair.

"Hmph, you must have been thinking about your ex!" he said mean mugging me. His whole demeanor abruptly changed from nice to nasty.

"No, it ain't nothing like that. I promise. I told you that shits dead to me baby," I pleaded.

"WELL EXPLAIN THE BULLSHIT ON THE SCREEN MUTHAFUCKA?" Jason said standing to his feet and pointing to the microwave. But only now, it wasn't a microwave. It was a television and on the screen was Desjardin riding my dick waving at the screen.

I frantically ran over to the T.V. or microwave, or whatever the fuck it was at this point, and tried to turn it off. The timer started beeping uncontrollably. I jumped up out of my sleep, which once again was a nightmare, to the sounds of my alarm clock. I scrambled to turn it off, but it fell on the floor. I got out of the bed, bent down to grab it, and turned it off.

I sat on the edge of the bed and rubbed my face. I have got to stop dreaming about this nigga. DAMN! What the fuck! I then remembered that it was Labor Day weekend and I was tasked to take Andre to the airport. He was going to go to Atlanta for pride. I probably should have gone with him, but I didn't really feel like dealing with 30,000 homo thugs right now although a distraction to break up the monotony could have been a good thing. Anyway, the family was supposed to be getting together and I was going to help Pops on the grill. It would be cool to hang out with the folks during these last days of summer.

I got up and walked to the bathroom to shit, shower, and shave. In the middle of shaving, I heard my phone go off. I ran back to the room to grab it. As I figured, it was Andre. I hit talk and put it on speaker phone.

"Hello! Gee! Wake yo' black ass up!" he said.

"I'm up, Dre. I'm getting ready now. Your flight is at 9:40, right?" I paused looking at the phone and then picked up the razor to start my shave again.

"No, nigga, 7:20!" he exclaimed. I stopped what I was doing to look at the clock on the wall. It was 7:11.

"Dre, you for real? I could have sworn you said 9:40."

"NO! I said 9:40!" he said breaking out into laughter."

"Aww nigga! I'ma fuck you up! I was about to say. I know I ain't going crazy," I laughed to myself.

"I know right? It was too easy, bruh. Say, did you call shorty the other night?" he asked inquiring about this cutie he sent my way.

"Yeah, we talked for a minute. That kat is dumb as rice. He just gon' be a piece of ass, Dre," I said.

"Well, damn bruh, that's all you need. Something to beat up, right?" Andre asked.

"Maybe so," I chuckled being careful with the razor. I rinsed it off under the hot water and applied the blade back to the section of my face I was working on.

"Yeah, just let shorty take the edge off. You need to focus on you for a minute anyway. All you need is some ass on a regular for now."

"That's easy for you to say. You and your nigga tight," I said glancing at the phone. I rinsed the razor under the hot water and prepared for the next stroke.

"Gee, you just got out of what a three-year relationship. Take some time out for you. Get this promotion and get in the homeowner's game. Fuck these niggas. Literally. Don't worry about what I got. You on a different chapter than me right now."

"I feel you, Dre," I said rinsing my face and turning the water off.

"Yeah, but are you hearing me? I need you to visualize some goals, and meet some deadlines for life. Stop tripping over Jason. If there was a way to get ya'll back together, as your boy, I'd make it happen. But for now it is what it is. Matter of fact there is still time for you to come with me to ATL shawty!"

"So you are going down there to fuck around?" I asked half-jokingly. I was checking my face out in the mirror making sure I didn't miss a spot.

"Naw man, just to hang with the crew. Catch a college game, do a little harmless flirting, see some booty's clap at that strip club we went to near Buckhead. Nothing crazy."

"Alright, Dre! Don't be me!" I warned. "Aw nigga I'm straight with what I got. But you need to get at shorty. Fuck his brains out and keep it moving. Clear your head and nuts," Andre said.

"I'ma see you in a few, Dre," I said laughing trying to end the conversation.

"Take heed man! Take heed!" he laughed. "Alright, hurry your Caribbean ass up. I'm ready to go."

I took a quick shower and threw some clothes on. I grabbed my bag and put a change of clothes in it, picked up an apple, my keys, and headed outside to my truck. I got in and tossed the bag in the back. I headed up the block towards the freeway to go downtown. Dre lived in the new Skybridge Condominiums they finished building a couple years ago. My boy was always on top of his shit. Tight crib, always drove the latest Infiniti, nice clothes, deep pockets. He was killing the real estate game, and finally found someone he was happy with. I knew he liked Jason, but never made a pass at him.

He told me one day after Jason and I were really serious, that out of all the things he has, that being with someone who wants him for him was starting to weigh heavy on his mind. It's amazing how love can change even a player's mind. Because Andre was out there but he was really diggin' Shawn and I was happy for him. Now I find myself wanting what he has. What a twist.

After I fulfilled my shuttle duties, I headed over to my folk's crib in Dolton. I was looking forward to seeing my little nephews David, Joseph, and Baron with their lil' bad asses. David was 12, Joseph was 10, and Baron just turned seven. Wanda and her husband Dwight had been doing pretty good. Wanda was now a professor at Northwestern and Dwight finally opened up his own auto repair shop not too long ago.

My younger sister Adrienne was doing pretty good as well. She was finishing up her master's in Criminal Justice. She was driven and focused on her career and was planning on applying with the Forensics Department for the FBI. Adrienne had been living in D.C. for the past three years. She always enjoyed crime solving and watched anything dealing with detective work. She'd tell us what they did wrong or how the various shows could have elaborated on something. Miss Detective was a trip.

Then there was my kid brother Timothy, a slightly shorter version of me. He was a couple of years younger than Jason and had just recently finished a B.A. in Advanced Computer Science. He was debating on moving out to California to work for a software firm. I'm not sure Mom would be too thrilled about that, but he and Adrienne both have been talking about moving out of Chicago in secret for as long as I can remember. We'll see what happens on his end. Moms may have let Adrienne leave, but Timmy is a big question mark.

Finally, Moms retired from almost 40 years of teaching and Pops was soon to retire in a couple of years. Pops was saying how he would like to go back to the islands and purchase beach front property for the two of them. Moms loved the island but was deeply rooted in the community here. I think she was cozy where she was. It would take a lot to up root her. She was still a feisty one. They reminded me of the younger Caribbean version of Ozzie Davis and Ruby Dee.

I made it over to the house and saw Pops outside washing Moms Mercedes. He was sitting on a step stool meticulously buffing the wheels clean. I parked the truck and walked up the driveway.

"What's happenin,' young man?" I teased. He had a big smile on his face as he stood up.

"Jus drying off yur Mudder's car ol' man. Maybe wit luck the rain will hold off," he said with his Caribbean accent.

"Pops, it's not going to rain. The weather should be good for a few days," I paused looking up at the sky. "It's going to be a hot one today though," I said.

"Yea, you may be right. Ya' feelin' all right?" he asked wiping his hands with a rag.

"Yes, sir, I'm good, Pops, why do you ask?" I said folding my arms.

"I know when sumthins troubling me chil'dran. Ya' got a sour look upon yur face dere son. Even though you smiling, I can see it dere," he said pointing his finger at my face.

"Pops, I just woke up not too long ago. I probably look sleepy or something," I said rubbing my goatee.

"Sleep an' stress is two dif'rant looks boy. Knowin' the dif'rance is wisdom. I don' forgot about more than you can remember son." he said shaking his head. "I'm good Pops, you need some help?" I smiled trying to change the subject. I guess I wasn't masking my hurt very well. Dre was right; I needed to snap out of this funk.

"No. I'll manage," he said stopping what he was doing to look at me again. He placed his hand in his pocket. "What you can do is go an' make sure Timmy is up so we can go ta' da market. Dey got a sale on shart- ribs at Jewel's. And prep dat grill."

"Alright Pops. I'm on it," I said.

"See ya' in a bit. Tell yur Mudder to check her list agin." He pulled a list out of his pocket and handed it to me. "I know she'll be forgettin' sumthin'," he smiled.

"Okay, Pops," I said. I took the list and looked it over. He turned back towards the car to complete his task.

I walked into the house and saw Moms in the kitchen with Wanda. Moms was prepping some chicken wings and Wanda was cutting up some fresh fish. There was a box of crab legs on ice sitting on the island of the kitchen. I walked over and kissed Moms on the cheek.

"Mom, Pops wants you to make sure you have all you need on this list. He just wanted to concentrate on barbequing and family today," I said. I gave her a firm hug and sat at the table. I sat the list on the table, grabbed a banana, peeled it, and winked at my sister.

"That man always trying to call me absent minded. Gary, the list is on the fridge there," she said pointing the knife in that direction.

"You sure this is it? That looks like a receipt to me," I said holding up the list Pops gave me. She turned around, looked at the fridge then over at me.

"Gary, I'm going to put you across my knee," she threatened. I winked at her and we both laughed.

"Where my nephews hiding?" I asked.

"Dwight is going to bring them over later. They're at the shop now playing with that old Chevy of his," Wanda said.

"Oh, okay. I bought them some toys yesterday," I said.

"It better not be any more water guns. I had to whoop Baron's tail the other week. He sitting there shooting water at a picture on the wall in his room. I was so mad," Wanda said.

"Umph! Lord have mercy!" Moms chuckled. "Gary, he come in the other day I picked him up from school, and he says, 'Nana, does Tina Turner borrow your legs?' I said 'what?' He says 'your legs look like Tina Turner's legs, Nana. They look sexy like hers. You must let her borrow your legs," she laughed and continued. "I says little boy, 'what you know about sexy legs?' He says, 'a bunch of stuff. I'm a leg man, Nana.' That little child is something to sit and understand," Moms said as we all broke out into laughter.

"No, he didn't Moms?" I said laughing.

"I'm telling you. Oh he tickled me something awful. He cute just like my boys were when they was his age," Moms said continuing in her laughter. It always amazed me how she could turn her accent on and off at times.

"Gary, Baron is a hot mess! I don't know where he be coming up with some of this stuff. I got my athlete, my book worm, and my comedian slash womanizer," Wanda chuckled counting the boys down collectively.

"Yeah, my lil' nephew the Red Baron is going to be a little heartbreaker," I said.

"I know hitting on his grandmother like he crazy. Little grown self," Wanda said.

"Yeah, he gon' be the one to watch. That's what's up!" I said smiling.

"Gary, don't you encourage that behavior," Wanda said. She threw a fish head at me.

"I knew I heard a lame in the kitchen. What's up big brother?" Timothy said. He walked into the kitchen and put me in a headlock. Wanda walked over and picked up the fish head and popped my forehead.

"Boy, you the lame living at home with your parents," I said as Moms and Wanda laughed.

"Gary, you know we can't compete with that. Everybody ain't able to get the old Benz, an allowance, and free room and board," Wanda said before sticking her tongue out at Timothy

"My baby boy can stay with me as long as it pleases him," Moms said. Timmy walked over and hugged her, collecting a kiss on the cheek from her in the process. Even though he was spoiled, he's always been a responsible go-getter, but what do you expect? He's the baby of the family. We all spoil his ass and make sure he's well taken care of.

"That's right, Ma. I just finished school and didn't ask for a penny. I can do that. You ready to go to the store?" Timothy asked pulling a light blue t-shirt over his athletic frame.

"Yeah, Pops want the grill cleaned first though," I said.

"I cleaned it last night. So we're good bro'. Your sister is still up there getting ready. She wanted to go too," Timothy said. "I'll be right back. I forgot my wallet," he said running off.

"We don't have all day to be waiting on her. Tell her she needs to come on," I said.

"I hear you talking about me big head," Adrienne said walking into the kitchen. "Good morning, everybody," she waved at us with both hands.

"Morning baby," Moms said.

"I know you heard me with them big satellite ears you got," I said.

"Boy shut up! What are you drinking?" she said grabbing my Roebeks juice cup.

"A polar pineapple smoothie," I said as she popped the lid to view the contents. "Don't be drinking from my straw. I don't know what germs you got," I said.

"The same ones you do, boy. You both come from the same hole you know," Moms said with a chuckle.

"You tell him Mommy!" Adrienne said sipping my drink.

"Yeah, but that was a long time ago Moms. Ugh you gon' get your nasty sticky lip gloss all on the straw," I smiled.

"Ha, ha, ha!" Adrienne sneered.

"Give my drink back woman," I said as Adrienne sat the cup back on the table and reached down to hug me.

"I missed you boy. How you been?" Adrienne said kissing my cheek and rubbing my head.

"I've been good beautiful. You?" I asked. She used her thumb to wipe away the lip-gloss left behind from her kiss.

"Great. I'm doing pretty well in D.C. You and Jason need to come and visit me when you two get some vacation time," she folded her arms. "Where is my brother-in-law? He still at home sleep or is he working?" She said as Wanda and Moms looked at one another.

"I don't know where he's at?" I said nonchalantly. "We're not together anymore," I wiped the straw off and took a sip of my drink.

"What! Oh my God why? What happened? I'm sorry, why didn't anyone tell me?" She said looking at Moms and Wanda. "Gary, are you okay pumpkin?" Adrienne asked rubbing my shoulder.

"Yes and no. I miss him. But I have to move on. He seems to have done it, so why can't I?" I said avoiding eye contact with her.

"Gary, you two were so cute together," she pulled up a chair and sat down. "Oh my God! No, not my homeboy? Did he cheat on you or something?" Adrienne asked.

"No, I did," I answered.

"You big whore! GARY!" she said reaching over and hitting me on the head. Moms started laughing.

"Hey now! I already feel bad about it. You don't have to hit me," I said glaring at my sister.

"Yes, I did. Somebody needs to knock some sense into that thick skull of yours. I email him all the time. He didn't make mention of ya'll breaking up," Adrienne said. She crossed her legs and leaned back in the chair.

"I guess he figures that's my place to tell not his," I said.

"I'm going to kick his butt if I see him. I can't

believe you messed that up," she shook her head and folded her arms. "Great job, Gary. Maybe I can hook him up with one of my lawyer friends in D.C. I know just the person too," Adrienne said nodding her head as she and Wanda smiled at one another.

"And you would do that too, huh?" I said flaring my nose up at her. Wishing she could use her power of persuasion to hook him back up with me.

"Maybe. You guys were so cute together though," she shook her head again. "I just knew I was going to see him this weekend. Thanks, Gary." Adrienne said rolling her eyes.

"Moms, you hearing this?" I asked.

"You would think Jason was her brother," Wanda laughed. "Girl, I miss him too though," she said looking at me with disappointment.

"I second that," Moms said with a great big smile.

"Ya'll ain't right at all! Man! Listen to ya'll. What about me? I'm hurt too," I said slapping my hand on my chest.

"That's your own fault," Moms said stopping what she was doing. She turned the water off and wiped her hands on the towel she had draped over her right shoulder. "Now I usually don't like to meddle in my children's love lives, but Gary, you need to face your demons and own up to your mistakes, baby."

"Ma, what do you mean? I am," I said feeling like a child caught with his hand in the cookie jar. I was shook at this point at Moms change of attitude.

"I'm going to say this, and I want you to listen, okay?" she said leaning back against the counter. She placed a hand on her hip. I nodded my head yes and prepared to get scolded. "Now you sitting over there looking and acting like a victim, you need to stop it. You have a pattern you need to break. Now when you broke it off with Camille to be with that strange boy Desjardin, I didn't like it, but I understood that. She didn't have the right business between her legs," Moms said as Wanda chuckled. "Then you cheat on Desjardin, and frankly, I believe that boy is bipolar. Hmph, I always told my boys to watch who toy box yah playin' in," she said in full Caribbean flair shaking her head. "And now you cheat on Jason. It's a mess you need to clean up because you got a problem with being loyal. You're selfish, Gary. You've always been selfish. When you were young, you wanted to play with everybody else's toys even though you had toys of your own to play with. When you got bored with them, what did you say, you remember?"

"I'd say they were broken or something was wrong with them." I smiled shaking my head. And she just explained my ex's behavior the other night.

"Correct. You were always looking for the next best thing. You don't know how to be loyal to what's in front of you, but people aren't toys. You just can't play with people and discard them when the newness wears off or when you discover they have what you feel is a defect."

"I know, but it's different this time. I   didn't mean for this to happen, and I really feel bad about what I did to Jason," I stated.

"Ah yes, Jason. Then you meet Jason," she paused, chuckled, shook her head, and pursed her lips before continuing. "You ran back from Atlanta telling me that you finally met the one. This is it, Moms. I'm in love this time, Moms. Now I must say, I agreed, but what gives you the gall to say this is different, child?"

"Right! He's got a broken heart with your name on it. Poor thing," Adrienne said poking my head with her index finger. "He's still family," Adrienne said. I gave her a mean look and told her to quiet down.

"Well, maybe it's the same, Moms," I sighed, thinking, Damn, Moms can always see through my bullshit and show me where I'm hiding it.

"Go on," she motioned.

"I've actually learned my lesson. I can't think of a time that I was ever bored with him. Deep down I felt like he could do better than me, Moms. But he chose me and I thought if I cheated on him and gave him a pass to do it back, then it would knock him down in my mind a few notches and we'd be on a level playing field. I kind of asked him that in a roundabout way after I did my dirt, knowing I can't share my baby with nobody. Maybe that was my way of testing him because I've been around the block and he hasn't. But I realized just how screwed up my thinking was. It doesn't sound right, or make sense, but that's how I felt. To me, he's perfect and all my dirt caught up with me and tainted what we had. But I need him, Moms. How can I make this right?" I said holding my head down. It was the first time I really put things in perspective. I didn't want to go into too much detail because I felt ashamed about catching something. In my mind, bottoms were the only ones who caught HIV and STD's. Shit, they the ones on the receiving end of the dick, so when some shit was passed on to me, it was just the wake-up call that I needed to stop fucking around just because I could. Honestly, I did cheat on Desjardin, but it wasn't with Camille...

"Well, son, now you can call him and figure that out with a clean conscience. You know him better than we do. My work is done." She walked over to me standing me up so she could hug and kiss me. She then turned around humming a tune and started placing the chicken in the large glass bowl full of marinade she had sitting beside the sink.

"I should call him and make sure he's all right and bring him a plate," Adrienne said.

"Bring you're mean butt on so we can get this meat and start grilling. All ya'll are traitors," I said shaking my head. Moms, Wanda, and Timothy all broke into laughter.

Standing My Ground...

"Jason, I want to thank you so much for helping with the event. Your ideas really helped out a lot," Jerome said. Jerome was Javi's best friend and head of the Poetic Expressions set. We were helping with the clean-up from the Slam.

"Thanks. I really had a good time with the whole thing," I said folding up some chairs.

"What are you up to tomorrow? You should come chill with us. I'm having a little barbeque in Humboldt Park," Jerome said. He glanced over at Javier and smiled.

"Javi will be there," Marisol said. She was a friend of Javier's' who had helped us set up. She was a femme Puerto Rican lesbian, who had been frequenting a lot of our events since she had broken up with her girlfriend. She and Javi would pretend to be one another's "beard" when they were forced to attend straight functions.

"What makes you think I'm concerned about Javi?" I asked. I tried to avoid direct eye contact with her as I smiled to myself.

"That smile for one. You light up like a Christmas tree whenever somebody says his name. I think you two would be good together?" she said. She elbowed Jerome who was nodding his head yes.

"I'll be glad when they stop frontin.' Just hook up already!" Jerome said walking two chairs over to the cart.

"Don't be messy all your life, Jerome," I said hitting him on the shoulder as he passed by me.

"I'm saying. You two are so obvious. You like him don't you?" Jerome asked. He folded his arms waiting for a response. Marisol walked over to Jerome and rested her left arm on his shoulder.

"I don't know. I mean... anyway we gotta get this place finished," I said laughing. My mind shot back to our day in the park. That kiss was everything. But in my mind, it wasn't him I was kissing.

"What ya'll over here laughing about?" Javi asked. He wheeled in another cart for the last of the chairs.

"You and Jason," Marisol said rolling her neck and pursing her lips like a ghetto girl.

"What about us?" he said putting his arm around me. He winked at me as he blew a bubble with his chewing gum.

"Shit, just the obvious. That this boy likes you and you like him," Jerome said. I stopped what I was doing and started blushing. The warmth of Javi next to me felt great, but I was reluctant to admit that I had any type of feelings for him.

"Ya'll are so bogus!" I said trying to stay inconspicuous.

"So is it true?" Javi asked smiling. Jerome and Marisol both looked at me with these cheesy grins. Marisol started nodding her head yes, as if she was giving me her blessing. "I don't know," I said not able to come up with a more age appropriate response.

"So you like Jason, right?" Marisol asked. Javi looked at me and then grabbed my face with both hands and kissed me. I wasn't expecting it, and admittedly, his spontaneity and aggression definitely grabbed my undivided attention. In my mind, I was definitely kissing Javi this time.

"Does that help you answer the question?" Javi said smiling at me. He was staring into my eyes. I was dumbfounded still not believing what had just happened.

"Aww shit ya'll nigga's is wildin'," Jerome laughed. He bit his fist and walked up and tapped Javi on the back.

"Ohhh! Blatino love at its best. You guys look so cute together," Marisol gushed jumping up and down like a cheerleader as I put a few chairs on the cart.

"This boy is speechless. Look at him," Jerome said as he dapped Javi up. "My man! You did that."

"You all right over there, Jason?" Javi asked still smiling.

"Yeah, I'm good," I was blushing. "We'll talk." I laughed. If I were Caucasian, I'm sure I would have been rosey as a juicy Pinklady Apple.

"I know. We should," he winked.

The next day I was on a plane to Dallas to check on my mama. I didn't know what to expect when I got there. I also didn't know if my dad was going to be home when I got there. I pictured all kind of things in my mind, like broken glass everywhere, moving boxes, and a sex tape playing. I didn't know what I would be walking into. All I know is that I wanted to see my mom, and make sure that she was cool. I told her that I was coming and that I would be renting a car. I didn't want to trouble her with driving the two hours from Killeen, Texas, to come get me.

Jasmine had been giving me updates on what was going on. She took the news pretty hard and wasn't sure if she could forgive him. She was Daddy's little girl, so this was a lot coming from her. And let's not mention her wondering how this would affect their granddaughter Aaliyah. She informed me that Mama was not saying much and that my parents had gotten into a couple of heated arguments the night before. A big part of me was glad I was out of the house.

It seems like every time I visited my family there were extenuating circumstances. There is always a funeral to attend or some tragic event such as this to get caught in the middle of. Nothing light hearted. Not only that, but I always have to mask who I am, guard my feeling, or play some stupid role to keep up appearances. I felt in my bones that this would not be one of those times to suppress my feelings. This trip was going to be the jump off.

The more I thought about it and the closer the plane got to the gate, the more my temper rose. I was amped but had to compose myself. Once we were parked at the gate, I unfastened my seatbelt and made my way to the baggage claim. I decided to use the restroom, wait for my bag, and then head to the rental car counter.

I made it to the carrousel which was already distributing luggage. I saw my suitcase and grabbed it. I then fumbled through my messenger bag for my reservation. With that in hand, I looked up and had to do a double take. On a bench not too far from where I was standing was my dad scanning the room. We made eye contact and I was stunned for a moment and couldn't move. I was not anticipating seeing him yet. I closed my eyes and casually made my way over to him. He stood to his feet and smiled as if all was right with the world. I swear I wanted to punch him. I thought I would have time to clear my head before seeing him. I mumbled to myself, Ain't this about a female dog!

"How you doing, son?" he said. He reached out to shake my hand hesitant to hug me. I guess he could sense my detachment.

"I'm cool," I stated plainly. What I really wanted to say was monogamous, and yourself? I looked down at my reservation trying to decide how to navigate my way through this situation.

"You got all your stuff," he asked.

"Um yeah, except my rental car," I said looking up at him.

"You don't need to rent a car. That's why I'm here. I wanted to pick you up so we could talk," he said.

"Talk huh?" I said exhaling slowly. I looked   to my left and flared my nose up noticing a family of four embracing one another and smiling with joy at the presence of their father.

"Yes, talk. I wanted to talk to you," he said. I looked back down at my reservation and against my better judgment placed the paper back into my bag.

"Okay, let's go talk," I said taking a deep breath. I made a mental note to be receptive of what he had to say. I thought back to what my mom had told me about him still being my dad.

I was really trying hard not to be disrespectful. Maybe I was prejudging him. It was hard, because at this point, I wasn't feeling him. I didn't want to ride with him and I was upset that he even bothered to come and pick me up from the airport. Worst case scenario, I could have Jasmine drive me to get a car later. I do not like being stranded.

We walked back to his truck like two complete strangers. This would surely become a highlight in our relationship I thought to myself. Two hours of me throwing shade. I put my suitcase in the rear cab of the truck and reluctantly climbed in on the passenger side. Everything within me was screaming go back into the terminal to carry out my original plan. So after about twenty minutes of me staring out of the window counting cow pastures, he broke the silence.

"How was your flight?" he asked.

"Good," I replied.

"So are you enjoying life in Chicago?" he asked. I thought to myself, REALLY!?

"Yes," I answered still gazing out of the window.

"How you doing in school? You're almost done right?" he asked.

"Yes," I replied even drier than before.

"Look, Jason, I know you mad at me..." he said.

"I'm not mad. I'm livid. I don't understand how you can do this to Mama. You preach all this stuff about being an upstanding man and claim to be an example of how I'm supposed to be, but you cheat on her," I paused and then continued. "With all due respect, that's a wonderful example," I said trying not to raise my voice. I looked at him awaiting a response. He switched hands on the steering wheel and rubbed his forehead.

"I hear you, son. Some things we do in life, one can't understand. Sometimes a man is going to be a man and do what he feels he needs to do whether that be the wrong thing or the right thing," he said.

"So what made you do the wrong thing?" I asked. I took a deep breath.

"Me and your Mama ain't been happy for a long time now, Jason. I don't know if you knew it or not. But we just haven't," he took a minute to breathe and looked over at me. "I'm through pretending!" He looked straight ahead at the road. "She wants to do her own thing. She can be cold sometimes. You know

133

how your Mama is. I'm trying to do one thing in the house, trying to save money, trying to do things so we can have something in our future, but she don't see it my way." He paused and glanced over at me. I diverted my attention in his general direction. "We have a lot of differences of opinions. And it's causing...it caused me to drift apart from her, son. It's days we walk around the house and don't say a damn thing to one another. I want a wife, Jason, not a roommate. And that's all there is too it."

"Well, have ya'll talked about that though?" I said. I was starting to lighten up a little bit. I didn't know just how deep things were even though I was still upset. Some of my anger stemmed from my own situation. I made an attempt to put my anger in check.

"Yes, we have, but it comes a point when talking isn't going to cut it. It comes to a stop. You can only address the same issues so many times without making any progress," he said pounding his fist on the steering wheel. "We have written letters to one another and talked, and wrote out plans. I even put it on the altar, but it's nothing if both people don't make the steps to change the situation," he said shaking his head. "So that's why you cheated. I mean, why not break it off before it got to that point," I suggested. "At least the terms of it ending wouldn't leave her feeling inadequate."

"Life doesn't work like that, Jason. A man reaches a breaking point and you fall victim to your own weakness. I messed up I know. It was a woman in the church and she offered comfort and a touch I wasn't getting at home. I regret it on the one hand, but on the other hand I don't, you know." He placed his elbow on the window seal and rested his head in his palm.

"So... have ya'll always been unhappy," I asked wondering how long the rift had been rearing its ugly head.

"Not always. It wasn't always like this. It's a lot of things that compounded on top of one another that caused this. I wasn't really ready to marry your mama." He glanced over at me and rubbed his head. "And I don't think she was ready to marry me. She was 18. She got pregnant and back then that was the honorable thing to do. You get married and make it work. I didn't want my kids to ever say I wasn't there. I didn't want to be that guy. The deadbeat. You understand?" he said looking over at me.

"I see your point," I said nodding my head. "So you got married because of me and have been unhappy for twenty-four years over something you didn't want to do in the first place?" I asked in utter disbelief. I didn't understand how you could fake your way through a marriage.

"No, not the whole marriage. And don't think you are the root of my unhappiness," he said reassuring me that it wasn't my fault. "I did it to provide for my family. I had to be a man and be there. That's why I

135

joined the Army and moved ya'll up out of a bad situation. Detroit for me was bad news. But with that, now I'm deployed or in the field all the time. So I think that also drove a wedge between your mama and me. Now we don't see each other for weeks - sometimes months at a time. She has free reign to live life as she sees fit. So when I come back into the picture to put my foot down and develop a game plan for my family, she don't hear what I'm saying cause she's used to doing things a certain way. What do you do?" He shrugged his shoulders and turned the AC down. "Then on top of that I feel guilty, so I let her do whatever she wanted to do with the money. Material things seem to make your mama happy," he shook his head and took a deep breath. "Keeping up with the Jones. It's deeper than me cheating main man. I'm telling you this as a man, cause you're my son, and hopefully you can learn from my mistakes."

"I see. You gon' be all right?" I asked hesitantly. I understood where he was coming from, but his actions were still in my eyes unjustified. I thought back to Gary for a second. My dad was expressing the same type of remorse that he'd felt, yet my issue with Gary was quite different in terms of how things played out. I thought to myself, I wonder if my mom and dad have been tested. Lord, please don't let either of them have anything.

"I don't know, son. My mind is heavy right now. My marriage has ended, my kids' lives are..." he paused and took a deep breath. "I blame myself son."

"Blame yourself for what?" I asked. He cracked the window, and reached in his console for a pack of cigarettes. I wasn't aware that he'd started smoking again. But with all that was going on, I guess I couldn't blame him.

"I blame myself...for you being the way you are. Jasmine getting pregnant. Hurting your mama," he rattled off. He lit his cigarette and took a long drag. "Maybe if I was there or could have done things differently, I could have a better relationship with my son and stopped you from liking men. All you had was your mama to look to," he said shaking his head. I sat there thinking, Ummm that's not the reason I like men.

"Dad, you or Mama didn't have anything to do with me liking who I like. This is me. This is my life. Not ya'lls. You don't have to blame yourself for me," I said. I knew at some point the gay thing would come up. I was always ready for it to come up with each conversation we had. We could be talking about how sunny it was outside, and he'd bring it up. I was tired of defending my quote unquote lifestyle.

"But you know it ain't right?" he asked. He took his eyes off the road to make eye contact with me. I held his gaze.

"Let me explain something to you, Daddy. This is me -take it or leave it. I didn't choose to be gay. Uncle Jesse didn't force this on me. You fighting for the country didn't force this on me. Me being around Mama more than you didn't force this on me. Me learning how to cook and clean up after myself didn't force this on me. This is me. I didn't wake up one day and say, 'You know what? I'm going to be gay. I want to drive a wedge between me and my family, and I want to be ostracized by all of society," I said doing a roundabout gesture.

"That is a choice, son. It ain't natural for a man to lay up with another hard leg," he said hitting the steering wheel. He was glancing back and forth between me and the road.

"Are you me?" I asked in a serious direct and stern tone.

"What are you getting at?" he said looking at me like I was speaking a foreign language.

"Are you me?" I repeated.

"No. I'm not you!" he barked.

"Well, please don't tell me about choices, Dad. Okay. It's taken me a long time to accept myself. MYSELF!" I yelled. "Just because you haven't accepted who you've become and the cards you were dealt," I paused and tried to bring my tone down. "You know what? You cannot live your life though me. It doesn't work like that. You can't relive your dreams or your youth through me," I said.

"Boy, I'm trying to tell you what God loves!" he yelled.

"If that were true then you would be telling me,

your son, that he not only loves you, but he loves me too!" I barked back.

"Jason, I will never understand why you would want to sleep with another man. It baffles me. I can't accept it," he said pounding the steering wheel. At that point I lost it.

"I wish ya'll could be me for a day. Just so you can get a glimpse of what I went through growing up. Ya'll never asked me how I feel about this," I   said getting my thoughts and words in order. I was about to go in, and he caught me on the right freakin' day. "I had a two parent home, both of ya'll should have been the model I would look up to as far as being a heterosexual, right?" He didn't answer. He kept his eyes glued to the road. I continued. "But those weren't the cards I was dealt. You and Mama don't even know me. You don't know my friends. You don't know my hangouts. Ya'll have never been to any of my duty stations or my home. And I've begged ya'll to visit me. Begged ya'll, Dad!" I paused for effect. "You don't know that I recently had my heart stomped on by my first love of almost three years. You don't know about my community involvement. You don't know about my writing. Ya'll don't know me! If you're going to blame yourself for anything dealing with me, blame yourself for that! As you can see you did a great job of raising me. Let's go down the list..." I said as he interrupted.

"Watch your tone boy!" he said.

"Dad, I'm not yelling. I'm just trying to get you to realize that yeah my life ain't easy. It's not easy being me. But in spite of it all, I'm connected to God first, I'm putting myself through school, I have my own mortgage now, and my hand ain't out begging for your support. I'm doing everything right! It's a shame that I have to beg ya'll to take the time to know me. This is not a choice. This is my reality. This is my life. Blame yourself for not wanting to be a part of it. The two of you are going to wake up one day and realize you never took the time to truly get to know your son. I have tried to open up to ya'll about more than this, but get slapped in the face. I don't blame ya'll for my sexuality. Ya'll didn't make me gay." I paused and faced forward. My dad sat there in silence as I continued my monologue. "I tell you one thing. From the looks of it, being straight ain't all that glamorous and full of happiness either. You two are the poster couple for that. Do you realize how much I hate coming home because I have to become this other person? So what is it going to take for ya'll to realize that you are losing your first born child to your own intolerance and ignorance," I said breathing heavily. I stopped my rant when I noticed that my dad had pulled off into a rest stop. I wondered what he was thinking.

He put the truck in park and got out. He walked over to a picnic table and continued smoking his cigarette. I debated on getting out of the truck or not so that we could continue our conversation. He's the one who said he wanted to talk. I rolled my eyes and got comfortable in my seat. I reclined and folded my arms. I decided to let him pout about the truth. I was done and I felt so much better now that I finally stood up for myself. He left the truck running. I thought about driving off for a moment but struck that idea down. I reached over and turned the ignition off. I made a mental note to have Jasmine run me to Enterprise so that I could get a car. If I knew where I was I would have gotten out and headed back to the airport.

After about twenty minutes, he came back to the truck. We didn't say a word to one another the rest of the way to Fort Hood, which was fine with me. I had said my peace, so now the ball was in his court. When we got to the house, I grabbed my things and made my way inside. Dad was on the phone probably talking to his sanctified Holy Ghost filled bust down.

I left my stuff by the door and went on a quest to find my Mom. She was sitting out on the back porch. My little niece Aaliyah was sleeping on a twin sized air mattress by the door. She was now three years old and looked cute as a button lying there. I took a picture of her with my phone. I opened the sliding door and stepped out on the deck.

"Hey, Ma. What you doing?" I asked.

"What it look like silly," she said smiling.

"You all right?" I asked as she stood up and gave

me a hug.

"I'm a little bitter, but I'll be fine. Thanks for coming down," she said sitting back down. I pulled up a chair.

"No problem," I said sitting down.

"Look at that crazy dog," she said referring to her Yorkie Terrier, Kirby. He was running around the yard chasing after a beach ball. It made me wish I had of brought Batman on this trip with me.

"A furry ball of energy," I said laughing.

"Where your daddy at?" she asked.

"On the phone out front," I said.

"Hmph. Hiding out, I guess. He ain't gotta sneak now," she said exhaling.

"So what's going to happen now?"

"We're splitting up," she continued to rock in her chair and looked over in my direction. "We've talked and we're going to go and talk to an attorney next week. I would have done it sooner, but I need to cool off. He doesn't even care." She threw her hand up in the air. "Just doing what he wants to do. All the shit I put up with, with him. All the years I stuck by his ass when he was doing his dirt in Detroit, and it comes to this." She took a pause. "He needs his space to grow. Nigga, you damn near fifty years old. How much more growing you need? He acts like he's Jasmine's age. What kind of mess is that?"

"Mama, have ya'll tried to work it out?" I asked.

"Jason, it's him. He wants this. I'm just going

along with his program. All we been doing all these years is trying. I'm the cause of his life not going where he wants it to go. I kept him from doing everything he set out to do. He the only one who's been hurt in this situation...hmph. Lord Jesus!" Mama said getting misty eyed. I had never seen her like this. She took her glasses off and rubbed her eyes.

"That's what he told you?" I asked.

"That's the gist of his side of the story," she sighed. She laid her head back on the chair and put her glasses back on. Kirby ran up on the porch and jumped in her lap. "Hey pookie wookie!" she said petting him. He jumped down and jumped up between my legs. I entertained him for a second and he was off to play with the beach ball again. There was a nice breeze brushing past us.

"Ma, have you eaten anything?" I asked.

"Not since the other day?" she said.

"You want me to fix you something to eat?" I said eager to come to her aide.

"Not particularly. Maybe later," she said glancing at me.

"Ma, were you two ever in love?" I asked out of curiosity.

"I was once...I don't know, things just changed. It was as if I was just in it to pass some time away. I love your daddy. I always have and I always will. I just pray I can forgive him for this hurt someday."

"Mama, did you marry him because you were

pregnant with me?" I asked.

"We got married because I loved him, and I thought he loved me. We were going to have a family. That's why we got married," she said. I wondered if she was just trying to spare my feelings. I appreciated her answer more than Dad's. I feel there are certain things you shouldn't divulge to your children.

"Oh. Okay," I responded satisfied with her response.

"Why you ask me that?"

"Nothing I just wanted to know if that was why ya'll married each other. Doing the honorable thing... you know?" I said with a quotation hand gesture. I smiled managing to bring levity to the situation.

"Jason, naw. We got married because that's what we wanted to do. I didn't pressure your Daddy to do anything he didn't want to do," she said.

"You gonna stay here?"

"No. I'm going to move. I'm not sticking around here. Jasmine is in school though, so I got to be there to help her out. Jason, I don't know exactly what I'm going to do right now, but I'm going to be all right. I'm not crying over this anymore. It's time to start moving on," she said.

"Well, I'm here for you, Mama," I said reaching over to give her leg a squeeze.

"You better be. But I don't want ya'll choosing sides Jason," she said pointing her finger at me. "This is me and your daddy's fight. Now ya'll are grown, so what ya'll choose to do with that is on ya'll. But you only get one father and one mother," she said with a stern look.

"I know, Mama," I said looking down at my feet. "I know you're upset, but this is what things boiled down too. Okay. I need ya'll to keep that in mind. Okay?" she said.

"Yes," I said. I think I was a little reluctant to hear that right now given the circumstances. Hell, I knew what she was going through.

"Look at me? I don't want ya'll to hate him or hate me for what's going on. This is our fight. Okay?" she was staring at me intently.

"Okay, Ma. I got it," I said looking at her and smiling.

"I know how you can be," she said. Aaliyah had awakened and called out to Mama. "Open that door Jason."

"Hey, little mama! You up?" I asked and smiled at her.

"Yes," Aaliyah said rubbing her eyes. She walked over to me and hugged me.

"Who is that stranger Aaliyah?" Mama asked smiling at her.

"You know who you hugging?" I asked.

"Unka Jason," she said smiling at me.

"Ah ahhh!" I said hugging her back. I picked her up and sat her in my lap.

"Mmm hmm. You my Unka Jason," she smiled.

"You sure I'm Uncle Jason?" I asked.

"Yeeess. I'm shuwah," she replied.

"Okay. You got me. I'm Uncle Jason," I said tickling her. "Did you have a good nap?" I straightened out the barrette attached to her little pig tail and kissed her on the cheek. She was a pretty little chocolate cutie with the biggest dough eyes and the sweetest demeanor I have ever witnessed from a child. That was my baby and from the moment I held her as an infant, it was love at first sight. Anytime I was around her, my paternal instinct would awaken in me as a need to shield her from this hateful world kept me on alert.

"Yes. I was over there. Did you see me?" she said pointing to the air mattress.

"Yes. I saw you over there. I took a picture of you," I said pinching her little chubby cheek.

"Ah ah! I was sleep," she said.

"I know. I took it while you were sleep."

"But you gotta be awake to get a picture taken Unka Jason," she said.

"I was up, but you were sleep," I said poking her stomach.

"OH! Okay," she giggled. "I gotta go potty," she whispered looking at my Mom.

"Okay, tell Uncle Jason to take you to go potty," Mama said.

"Unka Jason, I gotta go potty," Aaliyah said

bashfully.

"Okay, let's go, little mama," I said placing her on her feet.

"Okay," she said.

"Jason, wash her face too," Mama instructed.

"Okay, Ma," I said walking Aaliyah to the bathroom.

I stayed through the weekend. Jasmine and I talked about the divorce and I asked her how she felt about things. She was disappointed and felt like they should work it out. I reassured her that things would be okay, but our parent's relationship was non-salvageable. The damage had been done. I had lost a great deal of respect for my dad and wasn't quite sure how to get back to how things were. We didn't have the best relationship to begin with, but dang!

Mama told me that she'd be okay and that he was going to get his. I mentioned to her that she should go and get tested for STDs; I don't think that was at the top of her to do list. I stressed the importance of it, and hoped that she would take my advice. I asked her to tell Daddy the same thing.

In my heart of hearts, I could understand where she was coming from. However, I could see my dad's perspective of the reasons behind the split as well. My thing was he didn't have to dog her out like he did. To me, if he was such the man he claims to be, he should have bowed out gracefully a long time ago. 24 years is a long time to stay in a situation in which you're not happy. That's prison time with a free man's leisure, but at the end of the day I am very grateful he was around. A young black male needs male logic and influence in his life growing up.

In light of that, I set myself free and told him exactly how I felt in regards to my sexuality. I had a more tactful conversation with my mom concerning the same issue, and the general answer was the same as his. So at this point, I'm over it and know where they stand. They say they love me, but they will never understand or accept me being gay. That's fine with me. I know what boundaries I have with them, so the lines in the sand have been drawn as far as I am concerned. I tried. They need to learn you can't talk someone out of their own life...

Ups and Downs of Today...

It was so good to be back on my own turf. On the flight, I had plenty of time to reflect on the drama that ensued in Texas. Though it was a hard pill to swallow, my mom was right though when she said this was their fight. I had to keep repeating this to myself until it etched its place in my mind. There was nothing that I could do to help them mend fences. This was something that if they chose to do so, would have to happen between the two of them. At one point during the visit, I felt like a helpless kid wanting my mommy and daddy to stop fighting.

It probably didn't help matters with me adding my own dose of drama to mix. Personally, it was bitter sweet. All those feelings and emotions I had held onto for so long were released from my shoulders as if a stuffed tattered knapsack was strapped to my back. I was tired of beating around the bush. Through my own experience, I thought that I was going to be able to console my mom, which is why I rushed to her aid. I could relate to her in regard to having a cheating mate. However, I wasn't able to do so because of the closed minded views she has in terms of homosexuality. A gay relationship is a joke or not deemed real to some people including my parents. My personal life experience didn't quite measure up. Maybe I was still too young and too naïve. This sums up why I find it so hard to have adult conversations with my parents.

This one aspect of my life makes my experiences ambiguous and less meaningful when compared to their own life trials so much so that I don't share my hardships with them. I don't even share when I'm scared about life's challenges. I pray, hold on to faith, and keep moving forward. Ignorance in my mind has to be left behind. No longer will I live on the outskirts of His promises because of someone else's intolerance. That weekend, I learned that I am the child of two human beings, but I am not a child anymore.

As much as I wanted to trust them with more of who Jason is, it is just something that I wasn't and maybe will never be allowed to do. My attempts are always met with resistance as if the full form of the adult Jason doesn't matter. For so long because they were my parents, I had given them the benefit of the doubt. The reality they had to face was that I couldn't be controlled or manipulated any longer. I no longer viewed them with a child's eyes. I viewed them as individuals who were still figuring out life the same as I. They didn't have all the answers either.

In light of their dealings with me, maybe this was the breakdown of their relationship. I could tangibly see that they didn't know how to relate to one another because they never had the chance to know who they were as individuals. This causes you to love one another through glass walls. Looking back, there always seemed to be an elephant in the room where my parents were concerned. There was a palpable sadness that no one wanted to address. Let's just put on a brave face and sweep it under the rug. Our son's homosexuality, grab the broom. Our daughter's pregnancy, grab the broom. Our lack of tenderness towards one another and our children, grab the broom. Finally, the demise of their marriage. We each had lived in our heads for far too long. My sister and I walked around on eggshells, trying so hard to avoid the crap shoved under our family's rug. It's amazing I lasted this long. For the first time I had a new appreciation for my friends. They knew me, they got me, and the bond we had was genuine and brutally honest. It was so good to see them upon my return from Texas...

"Okay, you need to go first. What's the deal with this impromptu visit to Dallas? Who dick you suckin'?" Michael said laughing. "I smell dick on your breath."

"You smell Double Mint gum, slut bag!" I laughed.

"You're masking the smell. Whose dick was it? Come on now, spit it out," he said sniffing me. I pushed him away.

"I went to see about my mama, boy," I said. Michael and Preston had picked me up at the airport and we went to eat dinner at TGI Fridays near Midway Airport.

"Oh, okay, cause you know you will travel for dick," he said reading me. "What's wrong with your mama?" Michael asked reaching for a boneless buffalo wing.

"Chile, my folks are getting a divorce," I said sipping some water. That was the first time I said it out loud and it didn't sound natural for some reason.

"Shut up! No! Sweetie, are you alright?" Preston asked emphatically. He removed his eyewear, folded them, and placed them gently in their case.

"Yeah, I'm good. I'm just kind of feeling weird about it. I mean do any relationships last?" I said stretching my arms out in wonder. I looked at both of them collectively hoping that one of them had an answer.

"I know right? How is your Mom?" Preston asked.

"She says she's fine. She was torn up about it though. Ya'll it turned into the Boston Tea Party, do you hear me?! I spilled all my tea about being gay, and they spilled all their tea about the inner lining of their marriage," I took a sip of water and continued. "I let my poor Dad have it, but I didn't mean too." I said.

"Yes, you did," Michael quipped nodding his head. I rolled my eyes, and smiled recalling the conversation that took place in the truck. Perhaps Michael was right.

"Anyway hag! The point is it was a lot going on this past weekend and I'm over it, so... let's talk about Atlanta. Go!" I said concluding my portion of the conversation. I really didn't want to mull over this any longer. Preston rubbed my back.

"Atlanta was wonderful! You should have been there. It was a buffet of booty and ding-a-ling stew and chocolate cakes with extra syrup. Plus, I ran into my ex. You know the one you can't stand?" Michael said waiting for my response.

"Who, Kareem's 'ol late dyke looking self?"

"That's the one. I banged his back out the whole weekend and told him, 'Sure, we can get back together.' I only did it so he would keep the booty on ice for me while I was there. That was my break in case of emergency ass. His shit so tight; it feels like it's lynching my dick. Mmph!" Michael stated going off on one of his sexual tangents.

"You're going to be on the gay side of hell. In the section with no ice and all the bitter jaded lovers you've screwed over. You know that, right?" I said as Preston and I laughed.

"That's the price you pay when you don't follow the rules I set forth when in a relationship. I gave him several chances to just be real Jason. But he dug himself deeper and deeper. So I had to get him."

"Wow," I said in my Oprah voice. "As long as you can sleep at night, I'm not one to judge, but dang!" I said shaking my head. "And Preston you just let him do it."

"Chile, I didn't know. Honestly," Preston said slapping Michael a high five, shimmying, and concealing his laughter.

"Ya'll are a mess," I said laughing.

"This is him texting me now," Michael said. "Oh somebody is mad. He just said FUCK YOU NIGGA!"

"Well that's nice," I said sarcastically.

"Exactly!" Michael replied. "Thanks for the easy access to that ass. Send," Michael said out loud as he texted the boy back. I shook my head laughing.

"In other news," I said gawking at the guy walking by our table.

"Damn, he is phyne!" Preston said turning in his direction and craning his neck to look over the booth.

"Ain't he?!" I said slapping him a high five.

"Bottoms," Michael replied.

"Don't judge us," I smiled.

Michael dropped me off at home and I made my way inside. I brought my bags upstairs to my room. I called my co-worker Julia to let her know that I was going to be leaving out to pick up Batman from her house. She had a couple of Miniature Pinschers and did me the favor of taking care of him while I was gone. She let me know that she wouldn't be home until late that evening and that I could come and get him tomorrow after work.

I then called my mom to tell her that I finally made it home safely. She sounded about the same. Her tone was numb and cavalier. I knew from experience that it was going to take her a while to get over this one. I can't imagine being with someone faithfully for 24 years and then all of a sudden the relationship comes to a dead stop. My heart goes out to her.

I laid across my bed and relished in the silence. I was exhausted from all the fighting, the snide remarks, my flight, my thoughts, and from the previous work week. I hadn't had a moment to myself or a chance to unwind. I wished I had my dog to pet at least. I started to doze off when my phone rang. It was a number with all eights and I knew exactly who that was.

"So when you coming home, Dee?" I said answering the call.

"That's classified information their shipmate," Darius said chuckling

"How you doing? You alright?" I asked smiling.

"I'm all good, baby! How have you been?"

"I've been better, but I can't complain. Not with you over there," I said.

"What happened? You okay?" he asked.

"My parents are splitting up. I literally just got back from Texas tonight," I said trying not to sound like Debbie Downer.

"I'm sorry to hear that. Man, that's deep. Damn Jay dub, you good?" He asked.

"Yeah, I'm good. My mama is taking it pretty hard. How about I email you the details? I don't want to waste your card talking about that. What's going on with you? How are you doing?" I said.

"I'm pretty good, the research is going good and I am adding more experience to my resume. How is school coming along for you?" Darius asked.

"I'm doing good. I was supposed to be studying this weekend, but life happens. I have an A in my business communications class, and a low B in my healthcare concepts class," I said.

"Oh I'ma need you to raise that low B up to at least a low A. Get it together, bruh," Darius said.

"I know, I know. I'm going to get it together.

The class isn't over yet," I said.

"Yeah make it happen. How did your event go?"

"It went very well, Dee! The poets were so on point! This chick named Just Words won the show. She did a piece on the plight of a lesbian gangster. It was about her hustling in the streets perpetrating as a dude and overcoming adversity, after being raped by her crew and contracting HIV. It was pretty deep. I had a ball," I said.

"Did you bless the mic?"

"Yeah, I did a piece called, 'Positive Punches'. They received it well," I said.

"Oh yeah? You should send it to me. I'd love to read it," he said.

"I will do that. So have any of the dudes out there caught your eye?" I said smiling.

"I ain't gon' lie, there are some cuties out here. I'm not here for that though. I'm trying to do what I gotta do and get home. But it's crazy, because they have these down low parties out here. Nothing sexual, just like minds getting together," Darius said.

"For real?" I asked. "Yup! For real?"

"And you ain't checking for nobody out there?" I asked sucking my teeth.

"Nah, who you trying to get at?" he asked curiously.

"We not talking about me now, are we?" I said avoiding his question.

"Let me find out. I'm trying to claim that. Oh shit! Yo', baby I gotta go, one of the alert sirens just went off. I gotta get back. I'll try to call you back tomorrow. A'ight?"

"Okay. Is everything okay?" I asked startled.

"Hopefully so. I gotta go. A'ight?"

"Alright. Be careful. Bye bye."

"MUAH!" He said kissing the phone. I heard a click followed by a dial tone.

I got up and walked to my office to jump on the computer. I logged on to yahoo so that I could forward the poem to Darius and update him on my parent's dilemma. I was just about done with it, when I got an instant message from Gary's sister Adrienne. We were still really cool and were still emailing one another every so often. I was supposed to link up with her in D.C. next month. I had to attend a dental conference sponsored by the American Dental Association ADA. The chat went as follows:

I am so mad at you right now. Why didn't you tell me about you and Gary?

I didn't know how to tell you. I said.

OMG! Sweetie, are you okay? I was devastated when I found out.

It was devastating to me as well. I couldn't believe it. I'm good though. I said.

I can't believe my brother did that to you?

Yeah, I mean things happen. I said.

You miss him?

Yeah, I do sometimes. I still have love for him. That's not going to change, but the damage is done. I said.

Well I hope we can still remain friends.

Oh Adrienne, that's not going be a problem. I said.

Cool, well are you still coming to DC next month?

Yes. The same dates. I said.

Maybe I can hook you up with one of my friends out here. (WINK)

LOL! Cool. Looking forward to it. I said.

Alright cutie! Gotta get my beauty rest. TTYL

TTYL Love ya! I said.

I completed the email to Darius and hoped that everything was okay where he was. He had never had to rush off the phone like that since being over there. He kept telling me that it was not that bad where they had him stationed. He seemed to be in good spirits and kept his energy up which was good. I logged off and hopped in the bed falling asleep pretty quickly.

A Clean Bag of Health

I made a call to Michael to see if he was going to attend the little get together over on the South side with me and the rest of the judies. I hadn't heard from him nor had I seen him all week. We were all getting worried because this was unlike him. He is usually in the city on the weekends terrorizing the boys or hanging out with the crew. I decided to head up to Waukegan to check on him. I called on the way there to see if he would answer the phone. When I didn't get an answer, I really started to worry. It was going on five o'clock by the time I made it to his apartment complex. He should have been off work by now.

I circled the parking lot to check and see if his SUV was parked outside. When I saw it, I parked and headed up to his building. I looked up towards his balcony to see if I could see any light or signs of life. The place looked dark and the shades were drawn. I opened the front door and walked up the stairs to his unit. I placed my ear to the door and heard nothing. I knocked on the door. Nothing. I knocked again. Nothing. I then used the key he had given me to unlock the door. I pushed it open slowly poking my head in initially.

I caught a shadowy glimpse of Michael lying on the couch staring at the ceiling in complete darkness. The only light making its way into the room was coming in from outside through the cracks from the vertical blinds. He was wrapped up in a blanket and had a fan blowing on him at the highest level. The whooshing draft of air pushed by the blades and the hum of its motor were the only thing permeating the silence. I walked all the way in as he maneuvered his head ever so slightly to look up at me. His place was a mess, and the faint smell of old food lay heavy in the room. I walked over to one of the end tables and turned on the lamp.

"Are you in mourning or some tea, Michael? Are you sick, or did someone pass away?" I asked as I sat on the ottoman. I felt heaviness for my friend as I studied his face for answers.

"Yes. I died," he said avoiding my eyes. His facial expression registered no certain level of emotion.

"What the hell are you talking about? You're right here boy," I said trying to make sense of his comment. My soul was rattled at that point.

"I might as well be dead," he said. His statement was just as limp as his body appeared to be.

"Michael, what's wrong with you?" I asked genuinely concerned.

"Jason, I'm dying. They said I had to go on meds last week," he spoke motioning towards the dining room table. "So I took leave."

"Michael, is that all?" I said now pissed at him. I leaned over towards the table to observe the bottles. I picked up the largest one and read the label before sitting it back down. It really started to hit home that

Gary passed some crap on to me as well. I think that is why I was so pissed. This was becoming a vicious cycle. Someone infected my closest friend, scarring him for life which is why he has sex like an addict. And I get caught up by Gary and his ex. Thank God my case isn't as severe as Michael's, but it's still just as serious.

"That's enough, ain't it?" he asked. "I'm dying. They said my red blood cell count is less than 150, which means I'm a fucking AIDS patient now. They think there is a slight chance that the meds will bring it back up to undetectable levels, but they aren't fully positive based on the lab tests." He rubbed his chapped lips with his left hand and then let it fall to his side. There were dried tracks of tears on the sides of his face.

"You know what! Get your ass up off of this couch. I'm not going to feel sorry for you, and you aren't going to sit here and feel sorry for yourself either. Do you realize how blessed you are?" I asked. I jumped up and sprang into action, storming over to the patio door, pulled the blinds back, and slid the door open. I didn't want to face what could be a reality for us all if things keep going the way they are in this highly sexualized world we live in.

"Are you trying to kill me? It's cold outside," he said.

"Well then turn this stupid fan off," I said walking over towards him to move the fan out of the way. I shut it off abruptly. "You ain't doing nothing but blowing funky air up your nostrils. It's a wonder you aren't sick from that. It stinks in here! Get the hell up! I'm not playing right now! You got us all worried about you and you're in here acting stupid over something this small," I said debating on pulling the covers back. I folded my arms and continued as he finally made   eye contact with me. He looked stunned and confused as if I was speaking a foreign language to him. "Listen! You have more faith and trust in God than anybody I know. That right there should give you the hope that you need to overcome this. Taking medication and taking care of yourself properly is not going to hurt you. This is not a death sentence, Michael," I said clapping my hands together. "I can't believe you of all people are sitting up here sulking over something that will sustain your life."

"How are you going to read me about taking my meds?" he asked. He finally sat up and turned his body towards me. He kept the blanket wrapped around his waist. A tear fell from his right eye and made its way quickly to the corner of his mouth. He dabbed it with his tongue.

"The same way you did when I had the flu last year, that's how. I know the two illnesses don't compare, but the point is I don't like taking medication either, but guess what? When it's a matter of life or death, then you need to get with it and choose life especially when you are given a fighting chance. Start putting a condom on your dick like you preach to me, and limit the amount of dudes you mess with and your numbers wouldn't look bad," I barked.

"The doctor basically said I contracted a new strain of the virus. So now I got super AIDS," he said rubbing his face and sniffling.

"Come on, dude, you aren't built to give up!"

"Jason, you ain't the one who's positive! You're not dealing with what I am dealing with. You don't have to deal with being dizzy and constant diarrhea and the fatigue your body goes through. You don't know what I am going through," he said as another couple of tears ran down his face. He was frantically running down the list of things he had been subjected to in regard to HIV.

"I know, Michael," I said. I sat down next to him and calmed myself down. I was breathing heavy. I know all too well what it's like to want to give up on life, and I wasn't going to watch my closest friend go down that spiral. I also had another shot in a series I was forced to take scheduled soon.

"Not to mention the sadness of it all," he said looking down and rubbing his hands together anxiously.

"Okay, so you're depressed. And that's fine, but it's going on a week and a half, and you have been sitting up in this apartment giving up on life, instead of taking back what is rightfully yours. Your body.

That medicine on that table will help you do that," I said pointing at the bottles. "That and prayer, and the support of your friends. Your bothers," I said waving as if to say HELLO! "What are you afraid of? Why don't you want to take them?" I asked.

"Jason, that will be like admitting that I really have it," he said looking over at me. He rubbed his curly dark hair. "I've been fooling myself for so long because I haven't had to take meds. And now I have to fall in line with the rest of the positive people and become a statistic. I'm scared of how this will affect my career in the Navy. I'm scared of the side effects of the meds. I don't want to get the sunken in cheeks or develop a buffalo hump," he paused and looked back down toward the floor. "And what if the lab tests are right, huh? What if they don't work?" He said.

"What if they do? You have got to try," I said. He sucked his teeth.

"I know," he said as more tears ran down his face.

"Come here?" I said. We embraced and he really started sobbing. "It's going to be all right, Mikey. Better than you think, okay? You just need to change your diet, continue to exercise, take the medication like you're supposed to, and most importantly trust in Him."

"I will," he said taking a deep breath. I let him go. He grabbed one of the napkins sitting next to a take-out container and wiped his face dry. His face was just as red as his eyes.

"You promise?" I asked.

"Yes. I promise," he said trying to muster up a courageous smile.

"To take your medication and fight this?"   I asked.

"Yes. I'm going to take my medication," he said nodding his head.

"Good, because you know I don't do tears well," I laughed as I felt myself getting misty eyed. I thanked God He allowed me to break through.

"I can't tell," he said looking out towards the patio. I rubbed my eyes.

"Go get your butt in the tub. I'm gonna start cleaning up this pigsty. This is trifling, Michael," I said looking around. I picked up a container off of the table and showed it to him. "It's a wonder you don't have roaches living up in here," I said.

"I know right," Michael chuckled. He sighed and took a deep cleansing breath.

"Have you at least moved off of this couch?" I asked. I got up and walked into the kitchen and started cleaning up.

"Yeah to use the bathroom," he said.

"I'm surprised you didn't pee in the bottles surrounding the couch," I said.

"Shut up boy!" he laughed. He stood up and stretched his legs.

"I mean," I said clearing the sink. "And then after the place is cleaned, we can go and get something to eat. You need some sun too, with your high yellow tail.

"Jason," he said walking into the kitchen.

"Yes," I said without looking at him. I turned the water on and grabbed the dish detergent.

"Thank you," he said. He had a look on his face that came from a place of love. In that moment, my heart was warmed.

"It's what I do," I said shrugging my shoulders and smiling. "Now get your musty butt in the shower. Please! And hit them armpits two or four times. You smell like a bloomin' onion! And not in a good way" He laughed and headed to the bathroom. When I heard him close the bathroom door and turn the water on, I stopped what I was doing, closed my eyes and let out a quick sob. God, I didn't want that to be my reality.

A Burning Request...

I was debating on whether to lift weights or eat and watch a little T.V. I was on the night shift for Halloween. I was hoping it would be an uneventful evening. I challenged the board a couple weeks ago, and was still waiting for the results to come back. This promotion would take me out of regular field work and I would more or less be in charge of my own firehouse. I was really hoping to make lieutenant. I had devoted a great deal of energy towards my goal, and I was confident I would make it this time around.

I still had Jason on the brain, but not as much as I did before. I'd like to think I was starting to get over it. If I see him though I don't know how I'd react. Maybe we could develop some sort of friendship out of all this. On second thought, fuck that. That's my baby; I can't be that man's friend. I decided to lift weights to relieve some of my stress and then just relax for the remainder of the evening. I was hoping the citizens of Chicago would respect my request.

I walked into the locker room and started pulling out some workout gear from my gym bag. I noticed some old receipts at the bottom of the bag. I fished them out, and started to rip them up. I stopped myself when I noticed that one of the pieces of paper was a wallet sized picture of Jason. I smiled recapturing the memory of that day. We had decided to take pictures at this artsy spot in Andersonville. I was behind the photographer making silly gestures at him to get him to laugh. My walk down memory lane was cut short when the alarm sounded alerting the crew that a fire was present somewhere in the city. I balled the picture up and tossed it in the trash with the rest of the ripped up scraps of paper.

I threw my gym bag into my locker and ran to the equipment room to dress out. We were given the location, loaded up the fire trucks, and headed out. I jumped in the back and listened to the rundown of what was going on at the site. There was a massive fire in a high-rise building over on Cicero. The fire crew that was over there needed additional support and there were still some people trapped in the building. My squad and I were amped up and in rescue mode. My adrenaline was pumping. You never know what to expect when these fires occur. No one situation is ever the same.

My squad and I finally made it to the scene. We were given a quick debrief and I took charge dividing the team up into two search and rescue teams. We were looking for two young teenage girls and an elderly woman who was left behind. According to the daughter of the old woman, she was probably trying to gather up her photos. She said that she told her to forget about the albums and to come on. In a panic, she ran out thinking the woman was behind her. She assumed she'd gotten lost in the crowd. She was hysterical and I reassured her that we would bring her mother to safety.

The fire was somewhat contained as we entered the building with purpose. We couldn't completely extinguish the flames until all bodies were out and accounted for. The woman lived on the sixth floor which is where the fire started. We carefully made our way to that floor and called out to the woman to see if we could get a response. We entered the apartment and saw the woman lying on the floor with a towel draped over her mouth and nose. She was shaking very badly. I asked if she was all right to establish her responsiveness. She quickly nodded her head yes. You could see the look in her eyes turn from sheer terror to relief. I had one of the guys bring her out of the building.

I got a call on my headset telling me that the two girls had been found. I radioed back letting them know that we had the woman on the move. Our next move was to see if there were any other tenants on that floor. So we headed out to comb the remaining units. We walked into a couple of units and one of my guys, Billy, fell through the floor. Smoke and heat poured in through the opening. He was able to catch himself without falling completely through. I reached down to help pull him up. Right after I pulled him up and we were about to head out, I fell completely through another section of the same floor. I remember frantically reaching out for something to grip to catch myself. It was a feeling of complete helplessness as the smoke billowed past me blinding my view. I landed directly on my back. I heard a crunch as my lower back made direct contact with the base of my oxygen tank. I couldn't make a sound. I gasped for air and felt every muscle in my body tense beyond belief. I started to writhe in pain and heard the guys yelling for me. I started to black out and all of a sudden lost complete consciousness.

A few hours later, I woke up very groggy. I was wearing a hospital gown and looked down at my arm. There was an I.V. connected to me. I looked up and saw Moms walking over to me slowly with a warm smile. She rubbed my hand and bent down to kiss my forehead.

"You gonna be alright, baby," she smiled reassuringly. "Do you remember what happened?"

"I think I do. I remember a lot of pain and looking up at a big hole in the floor... yeah, I was fighting a fire looking for more people," I said.

"Do you feel something? Pain perhaps?" Moms said.

"I don't know. Am I paralyzed?" I panicked. I was hoping this was another one of the dreams I'd been having.

"Look down at your feet and wiggle your toes," she said pulling the covers back. I did as she asked.

"Oh thank you God!" I said with a sigh of relief as Moms laughed.

"You're going to be fine. The doctor says you ripped the tendons of the iliac muscle on the right side. It was the way you fell. So your pelvis is out of line. They say you also got some tissue damage of the lower lumbar region with a lot of swelling," she said.

"Is that why it feels so numb around my waist and back? My leg is all tingly," I said. I was trying to make sense of the injuries she described.

"Could be. They put you on some pain killers. You were out cold for a couple of hours now. I'm going to go get the doctor, sweetheart. Okay?" She said kissing my forehead again. She smiled and gave my hand a motherly rub.

"Okay," I answered thanking God she was here with me.

"Your father went with Wanda to pick up the children, so they should be back any minute now," she said.

"Okay. It will be good to see them."

"I'm coming right back," she said. "Okay, Mama," I said.

I pulled the sheet back again and wiggled my toes once more to double-check their functionality. I made an attempt to move my waist and slide up a little higher in the bed. It was an uncomfortable maneuver and I could feel a weird jerking sensation on my right side. It was like something was not quite attached. This is all I need right now -to be crippled or an invalid.

I had to pull it together and just wait to hear what the doctor had to say about my condition. I made up in my mind that this was not going to get me down. I placed my hands behind my head, and this proved to be a bit uncomfortable as well. I felt a slight tinge of pain as I moved from that position and folded my arms. It felt much better resting them there. Moms returned with the doctor and my baby brother. Moms was big on juicing, and she removed a container of fresh orange juice from her purse. She opened it and handed it to me with a straw. The doctor, who came in behind them, was an attractive athletic older Caucasian female. She was carrying a few forms and a pen.

"Mr. Larrieux. Good evening. I'm Dr. Weingard. How are you?"

"I don't know, lay the news on me," I said mustering up a smile. She smiled and wheeled a computer screen over near me so that I could view the monitor.

"Okay, well I ordered a Magnetic Resolution Image, better known as an MRI scan so that we could detect any damages to the spine or muscles of the pelvis. You were in and out of consciousness and you were complaining of pain in that general region. Now, let me just pull your chart up on the screen here and I can explain the findings," she said keying in my information. A series of images popped up. "Okay, so what we have here is a 3-D image of your pelvic region. You have a partial thickness tear of the iliacus muscle here along the femur. You also have a partial thickness tear of the psoas major. Now together these muscles are a part of a group commonly referred to as the iliopsoas. The iliacus is important for lifting or flexing the leg forward. The iliopsoas helps to bend the trunk forward such as sitting up in bed or doing sit ups."

"So is that why I feel a weird popping feeling?" I asked.

"Yes, the iliacus attaches to the inner portion of the hip bone as you can see here, and the psoas major starts here around the inferior spine making its way down here to this part of the femur. So what you have is a deviation of the pelvis. In layman's terms, one leg is going to feel longer than the other for a couple of months until things heal."

"So what is the healing process?" I asked scratching my head in not only confusion, but frustration as well.

"Well, you will definitely need a lot of physical therapy to assist you in walking and doing the simple everyday tasks of getting out of bed or bending down to grab something off the floor. Things to avoid are stair climbing, running, lifting, doing anything strenuous. You need to be careful on your right side. I am going to prescribe an 800mg Motrin and Vicodin for the pain. We'll get you set up for physical therapy as well. Do you have any questions for me?" she asked.

"So it's going to be painful to walk?"

"It could be. That's why you need to take it easy for the first few weeks. I don't want you to baby the area. Just use good judgment and be careful. The tendons will mend themselves, but it's going to take a few months to be back to normal. So initially, you'll need to rest in bed and take your medication as prescribed. You're going to be fine," she said.

"Thank you, Doctor,"

"Now we'll keep you here for a couple of days just to monitor things. So with that being said, I'll leave you to your family."

"Okay, thank you for your help."

"So let me know if you have any questions. I'll be around." She handed Moms her card.

"I sure will," I said.

"So what happened, how in the world did your clumsiness cause you to fall through the floor?" Timothy asked smiling.

As much as I appreciated my family being there for me, there was one element missing. Jason. I hate to keep harping on the fact that he's gone, but its times like these that I need his strength and touch the most. He knows exactly how to take care of me when I'm sick. I would nuzzle up under him when I wasn't feeling well, and he would just lay there for hours with me rubbing my head so gently. Any pain or headache I was experiencing from a long hard day or week of firefighting was worth the comfort my baby would give me.

I confided in Wanda how much I missed him and how I needed his touch. I needed to know if he still cared for me. I needed for him to come and make everything all right. I needed him to kiss me and need me in the same way that I needed him. How much time will it take for this void to be filled? I'll do anything to change his mind about us. I'll do whatever it takes; I need you right now, Jason.

Is My Man Okay...

"I love the sound of steady rain," Javi said.

"I know right, it's so calming, huh?" I said walking back into the room from the kitchen.

"Yup! This is a sexy set up we have here. And the rain is adding to it," Javi said.

"This was a good idea. I needed this." We were at my place listening to some music and talking. I had a bunch of candles lit, some wine, cheese and crackers, and fresh fruit set up on the table. I also had a set of oversized beanbags to lounge on. I pulled my shirt over my head and grabbed some fruit before popping a squat. Javi had convinced me to utilize my fireplace and that added to the ambiance as well.

"So you had a good time at the party?" Javi asked massaging my shoulders. I was sitting on a bean bag in between his legs and he was sitting on the couch. I popped a few grapes into my mouth and allowed myself to become putty in Javi's hands. At some point, I was going to have to let go and trust someone again.

"Yeah, it was good. I had fun. I wasn't expecting Jerome to be in drag. I didn't think he would ever do anything like that," I laughed.

"That boy is a fool. He'll do anything to get a laugh," Javi said.

"I know right? Banshee drag at its best. Did you see them knobby knees of his?" I said continuing to laugh. I will never forget how ugly of a female he made.

"I saw them. We've been teasing him about his knees since high school," Javi said. He worked his fingers firmly down my spine.

"That feels really good," I said closing my eyes. I rotated my neck and started rubbing his right foot. He stretched his leg out to give me greater access.

"That's what I do. I got something else that feels good too," Javi said.

"And what might that be?" I asked. The crackles of the flames were in sync with the soloist crooning a slow jam through the speakers.

"This right here," he said pulling my head back and planting a soft, juicy kiss on my lips. I opened my eyes and smiled. "What did you think?" He smirked.

"I likes, I likes. Give me more," I said. He leaned back down as if he were going to kiss me again, but moved to my ear.

"You'll get more wet kisses later," he teased.

"If you don't put me to sleep with this massage," I said.

"Trust me, you won't be sleeping," Javi said. I did a little shoulder bounce and bit my lip as he kissed my forehead.

"I'm glad you're here. This is cool," I cooed. But you ain't getting no booty tonight, bruh, I thought to myself.

"I hear that, papi. It's about time you let me stay the night," he said.

"I know; it's complicated. You know my situation," I said.

"If there was a situation, you wouldn't be up on me like this," he said. He ran his hands down my chest, grabbed me around my waist, and pulled me up. I stood up as he lay back on the couch and placed his hands behind his head. I slowly straddled him.

"Maybe you're right," I looked at him and smiled.

"I know I'm right. Talk to me. I see the wheels turning," he bit his bottom lip seductively.

"I've just been thinking about all kinds of things. Like, I could move and start over in a new city and focus on my writing," I paused and gently placed my hands on his chest. "You know, or go on some type of sabbatical. Maybe make a pilgrimage back through Europe or some artsy place and just write. Let my hair grow all wild," he smiled and grabbed my hands kissing them. "I'm dreaming I guess."

"Well, there's nothing wrong with that. Dreams can be reached. But you really gonna leave Chicago after you just purchased some property?" he asked.

"I just need a change of scenery. Like some place by myself for a couple of weeks. I don't know. I don't think I'll move. I've just changed so much; you know?" I said trying not to avoid his eyes.

"Yeah, it happens at various stages in life. You start to look at your life and see what it is that you haven't accomplished. You start doing a self-evaluation of you, your worth, and your purpose. Many of us just exist, but you are living life. I mean you need to do you, papi. Just make sure I'm in the picture somewhere," he smiled poking me and winking his eye at me.

"Oh so you want to do me too?" I chuckled and pinched his nipple.

"Yup!" he said nodding his head like an excited little boy.

"Hmmm..." I said staring into those dangerous bedroom eyes of his.

"Que paso?" he said winking at me.

"Nada. You're sexy as hell!" I said. I traced his lower lip with my index finger.

"I know I am. I'm Puerto Rican, I can't help it," he shrugged.

"You conceited bastard you!" I laughed. "Must you live up to the stereotype?" I thumped his chest.

"Sex appeal is in our DNA chico. Sorry," he said with pure conceit.

"Oh my God. What am I going to do with you?"

"Get rid of that other kid you checking for, stop thinking about moving, and fucks with me," he said. He ran his fingertips down my chest before resting his hands around my waist. He strategically placed and slid his hands partly into my pajama bottoms.

"It's that easy, huh?" I asked.

"Yup! It's that easy. You thinking about ol' boy in Iraq, huh? Don't lie either," Javi asked squeezing my booty. I grabbed his hands and placed them away from the red zone.

"I mean, I can't lie about it. Darius is in my head. But for one we live in two separate cities and I hate D.C. And we have this friendship that I don't think should be tampered with. Then there is you. I'm feeling this. I like this. I like you. But..," I said tapping his nose with my finger.

"But...?" Javi said.

"But I don't want to hurt you because of my own fears and hesitation," I said looking down at his chest.

"And...?" Javi smiled.

"There is no and. Well, yes it is," I laughed. "I don't need to be hurt again." I said.

"Well, that's why I'm here to be that guy in your corner. I'm not trying to hurt you. I'm not trying to rush you. I'm trying to be patient and get you on my team. I'm not going anywhere," he commanded my attention by lifting my chin up, so I could make eye contact with him. "You got me papi?" Javi said.

"That could be why you're here," I smiled.

"¿Donde es Javier? ¡Justo antes de los ojos!" he said.

"In front of my eyes, right?" I asked, making sure I had translated the Spanish to English correctly. He was teaching me every chance he got.

"Yup!" he said slowly shaking his head yes.

"I see you."

"!Le arrebatar hasta mientras se puede   chico!" he said.

"What does that mean?" I asked. "Snatch him up while you can," he said.

"Oh yeah, to snatch. See I'm learning. Okay let me answer. ? Lo que usted intenta hacer conmigo?" I asked.

"Good question. I'm trying to be the only dude to get your juices flowing. You'll fall for this kid right here," Javi said winking at me.

"So cocky," I said.

"Quisiera usted mucho," Javi said.

"Um...? Te gusto?" I smiled.

"! Ay si! ! Dame un beso!" Javi said.

"I know what that means," I smiled. My dick started to stiffen.

"! Besame! He said showing that sexy smile of his. I leaned in and we started kissing. His lips felt so good.

We were just getting into it when my phone started ringing. I reached over and grabbed it off of the table. I checked the caller I.D. I hadn't seen that number for quite some time and it startled me. I interrupted the intimacy to answer my phone.

"I'm sorry Javi, let me see what this is about," I said looking at my phone puzzled. I rolled my eyes and looked at Javi.

"You alright?" He asked rubbing my arm.

"Yeah, excuse me for a minute," I said hitting the talk button. I moved off of Javi's lap and sat next to him on the couch. "Hello," I answered quickly.

"Hi. This is Jason, right?" A female voice asked.

"Yes, this is he. Who am I speaking with?" I said barely recognizing the voice.

"Jason, this is Wanda. How have you been, sweetheart?" she asked.

"Oh hey, Wanda. I've been pretty good for the most part," I said wondering why the hell she was calling me.

"That's good. Um, were you busy?" she asked.

"Well, yes." I said turning away from Javi. He had stretched out on the couch. He crossed his legs over my lap. I started playing with his toes. "What's going on?"

"I'm sorry, Jason. I'll make this brief. Um... Gary was in an accident and... "

"Oh God! Is he alright?" I asked. My heart skipped a beat. I immediately started thinking the worst. I hoped he wasn't hurt or suffering.

"Yes, he's fine. He had an accident at work fighting a fire and hurt his leg and back really bad."

"Wow. When did this happen?" I said relieved that he was alive at least.

"Halloween night?" she answered.

"Is he still in the hospital?" My first instinct was to get up and immediately head to the hospital; I needed to see him for myself for some reason.

"Yeah, he should come out in a few days. He had a lot of swelling in his lower back, and they want to keep an eye on him," she said.

"Well, I hope he gets better. Oh my God. I'll keep him in my prayers," I said out of sympathy and love.

"Yeah, he'll need that. Thank you," she said.

"Oh no problem," I replied.

"Listen, I... well... he's been talking about you and I know he misses you. Now you're not obligated, but I think it might do him some good to see you. I mean, I know it might be a hard request. But it would mean a lot to him if you showed up," Wanda said.

"Um... sure, I could come through and see him. I don't know. Maybe for a minute or two," I said shrugging my shoulders. I glanced over at Javi. He was staring at me, patiently waiting for me to get off of the phone. I was feeling uncomfortable having this conversation in front of him.

"Okay, thank you, Jason, that means a lot to me and I know it will make his day," she said.

"Cool. Can you text me the information?" I asked without hesitation.

"I sure will. Well, I will let you get back to your evening. Again, thank you so much, Jason. I know it's a lot to ask," Wanda said.

"No problem, Wanda. You have a good one."

"Good night," she said.

"Good night," I said sitting the phone down.

"What was that about?" Javi asked.

"You are not going to believe this," I laughed. I thought about lying by not mentioning Gary, but opted to tell the truth.

"What?" he asked. I turned my body in his direction resting my arm on the sofa back.

"That was Wanda, my ex's sister. Apparently, Gary was in a pretty bad accident at work and has been asking about me and junk. She asked if I could visit him and wish him well," I said.

"That's pretty bold, huh? You gonna go and see him?" Javi asked nonchalantly.

"I don't know," I said as my phone beeped. It was a text from Wanda with the name of the hospital and his room number. My mind was saying, Hell yeah, I'm going to see him, though on some level I felt guilty about it. I still cared for him, yet I didn't know if this was something I should tell Javier.

"Well if you want me to go and offer some interference to get you out of there, I'll go with you," Javi smiled.

"You would too, huh?" I asked. I was more or less thinking to myself, how tacky and inappropriate that would be. It definitely wasn't necessary. Suddenly the thought of Javi being there in that moment made me question what the hell I was doing laid up with him while my baby was lying in a hospital bed?

"Of course. This way he can see that you don't need him because you got this phyne ass Boricua loving you down. You got me?" he said pulling me on top of him.

"That might be cool," I said. I wanted to go that night and comfort him like I did when he had a hard day at work, but then again, maybe that would complicate things. So many feelings I thought were gone surfaced just that quickly. "I need you to leave," I said out of the blue. My comment seemed to stop everything as the last song on the play list hit its last cord.

"You want me to leave?" he laughed lifting me up to get a full view of my face. It hit me as I realized what I had just said to him.

"Javi, I'm not being fair to you. I still need closure and I can't move forward with you until I figure out what, who, and where I want to be. I truly apologize. But I need to go see Gary. Now."

"So you just... damn, you aren't even going to give me chance... I'm here, where is he?" he said. He was pissed off and confused.

"In the hospital hurt pretty bad, Javi, I need to be by his side. I don't know why, but I've got to go. I need to figure this all out and you need to... I'm asking you to please give me time," I said getting up from the sofa.

"Alright, papi. Whatever you say. I don't like it, but I have to respect that," he said shaking his head and exhaling with a deep sigh. He grabbed his boots and stuffed his feet into them before pulling his sweater over his head. He then stood up grabbed his keys and wallet and I walked him to the door. He retrieved his fitted cap from the hook in the foyer and placed it onto his head. I placed my hands in my pockets, as he made his way to the door. I didn't know what to say.

"I'm sorry, Javi. I truly apologize for this random turn of events," I said with soulful eyes. Javi reached for the door knob before turning back to face me. He took a deep breath, his jaws were tight and he looked like he was getting angry.

"You just make sure his punk ass sees what I see, papi. You understand me?" I shook my head yes. All of a sudden he pushed me up against the wall and kissed me forcefully. "Damn, Jason," he said shaking his head. He turned away from me and headed out of the door. I watched him get into the car still feeling his lips on mine but feeling nothing from the kiss but a longing for that to have been Gary. I couldn't lose him. I had to go see if my man was okay.

There Goes My Baby...

Although it was nice to do absolutely nothing, I was getting tired of lying around the hospital. I had been here for almost a week. This shit was starting to be for the birds. And it was raining outside tonight. The good news is I only had a day left before I could go home. The doctor wanted to take extra precautions with me because of the swelling that had formed around my lower spine. I was on medication to help it go down and it finally looked to be working, but there was still a lot of tissue damage. My leg was killing me at times and was really stiff. I was rolling with it though. They had me doing a few stretches with a band three times a day. The doctor said it would help restore mobility.

I really just wanted to be home or at work and enjoying life. Everyone had come to see me. My fire chief and crew, all my niggas, and my family had come through and really showed love. There were flowers, balloons, stuffed animals, and shit everywhere. I smiled thinking, that's what's up! I noticed a new card on my little table. I reached for it and opened it up. It was a card from my nephews. It was one of those cards with sound. It had a picture of a fire truck racing down the road with sirens blaring. It read: Wishing you a speedy recovery! They each wrote out "Get well, and we love you, Uncle Gary." My youngest nephew Baron added: "P.S. My leg hurts too, Uncle

Gee," and he drew a little sad face. I laid my head down on the pillow and closed my eyes for a second. I heard a knock on the door. I opened my eyes, looked up, and to my surprise it was Jason... for real this time. He was standing there looking good as a muthafucka! He was wearing some fitted gray jeans with a tasty looking sag, a fitted white and red V-neck tee, a jean jacket with a red hoodie attached to it, and a crispy pair of red and white sneakers from Aldo. He was growing his hair out and had a tapered cut. He was all clean shaven. I thought my mind was playing tricks on me until I heard his voice.

"Good afternoon, sleepy head?" Jason said smiling. He looked as if he was debating on whether to come in or not.

"Oh shit! Look at you? What's up Jason? How you doing, babes?" I said barely containing my excitement.

"I'm good, but how are you?" he asked. He walked up to the side of the bed.

"Is that for me?" I asked.

"Oh yeah, my bad. I brought you an Edible Arrangement and a card. I know how much you love fresh fruit," he said smiling. He reached over and pulled my tray table in front of me and placed the basket on top. I couldn't help but to take a sneak peek at his plump back shots as he reached over to reposition the table. He had on a pair of red and blue striped underwear. I felt my dick begin to swell as the thought of caressing that ass crossed my mind. I wanted to put the wood and the mustache back there at that moment. "Thank you. I appreciate that," I said grinning looking back into his eyes.

"Cool. You're welcome. So, how are you feeling, Gary? And what the hell happened?" Jason asked. He folded his arms awaiting my reply. There was something familiar yet different about the way he said my name.

"I fell through the damn floor doing a sweep of a building we were trying to secure. All I know is I was stepping out of one of the rooms, and I lost my balance. I landed on my back in a different apartment. I guess the way I fell most of my weight was on my left leg. I tore up the NBC, ABC, 123 and idiot ligaments in my knee, some shit the doctor said. I just found that out a couple days ago." I smiled as Jason chuckled at my silliness. He reached over and touched my knee. "On top of that I had a lot of swelling in my lower back, which they say has my pelvis out of whack. It's putting pressure on my spine. I tore some ligaments in my lower back also, so they are keeping me here for observation," I said opening the basket.

"Man! That's crazy dude!" he paused and looked at me with gentle compassion in his eyes. "Well, I'm glad you are doing well. I was thinking it was worse, but thank God you're okay," Jason said. As comforting as his words were, it sounded as if he didn't really know what to say.

"Nah! It could have been though. How did you know I was here?" I said shoveling grapes into my mouth.

"Channel Wanda! Action news!" Jason laughed. He gestured a frame with his hands centering me as the subject.

"Is that right?" I laughed.

"Yeah, she told me you had been in an accident and that I should come and check on you. So here I am. You know she can't hold water. She called me the other night," he nodded his head and folded his arms again putting up his guard.

"Damn. That's what I'm talking bout! I'm so happy to see you." I took a moment to stare at him. "I'm glad you came, babes," I said smiling. I could tell he was battling the nervous energy brewing inside of him.

"No problem. Despite what you think, I still have some level of compassion for your butt," he said reassuring me.

"For real?" I asked.

"Yes Gary. For real." Jason said.

"Well you look good boy. I see you still taking care of yourself. What you been up too?"

"Thanks. Um... Just work, school, and grown up stuff," he said with a nervous laugh. He rubbed the back of his head. "I bought a little crib on the North side. I'm doing pretty well."

"I heard. Andre was telling me about it. I'm happy for you. It's a big step to do on your own," I said.

"Yeah, I know right. I put my VA loan to good use," he smiled. Did you get your promotion yet? I know you were working hard on that," he asked.

"Not yet. I'm still waiting for the results. I did my board not too long ago, so it's just a bunch of hurry up and wait right now. You still working at the same place?"

"Yeah, and then some. I applied for a government position at the base. It will mean more money. Doc is scaling back, so I'm working at two different offices to keep my change from looking strange," Jason said laughing.

"You talking about the Naval base?" I asked.

"Uh huh. I applied there, but there is a spot opening at the Marine Reserve In-processing Center. That will keep me in the city, so I won't have to commute," Jason said.

"I know. With gas prices, that'll be crazy...plus wear and tear on that new car you got," I said tapping his arm.

"What new car?" Jason blushed.

"Andre told me about that too. What you end up getting?"

"I can't have no business, huh? As big as this city is?" Jason said laughing and shaking his head.

"Hell naw! This is my city. You know nothing gets past me," I said.

"Whatever. His homeboy Travis hooked up a good deal for me on a pre-owned 3-series," Jason said.

"Oh shit, you upgraded?" I laughed bringing my fist up to my mouth.

"Yeah, I'm trying to do a little sumthin' sumthin'," Jason smiled looking away from me. He turned to look at the IV bag next to the bed.

"So you finally got your lil' Bimmer!" I smiled. "You gotta give me a ride one of these days."

"That'll be cool," Jason said looking back at me. He had a shy and modest look on his face. He was still as beautiful as I remembered.

"Still the hot boy! I see. Lil' bachelors pad, new ride. I'm glad to see you doing the damn thang," I said wishing I were still a part of the equation.

"Yeah, which is why I need to keep an eye out on these positions on base. I worked hard for my junk. I just thank God," Jason said.

"I wouldn't even worry about it. Either one of them jobs are as good as yours. It's the healthcare field."

"Yeah, we'll see what happens. I don't want to get to cocky thinking like that. You know there's a shift beginning to happen in the economy, so I need some security," he said.

"With your trade, you'll always be marketable though. What are you going to school for?" I asked.

"I'm taking up health care management. I'm going to go ahead and finish this last year and a half," Jason said. "I need something to fall back on."

"I feel you," I said.

"How are your parents doing?" Jason asked.

"They're doing real good. Pops finally retired and Moms is soon to follow. Everybody is good though. What about yours?" I asked.

"They're going through a little hiccup right now. They are about to divorce, so it is what it is," he said shaking his head.

"I'm sorry to hear that, Jason. Damn," I said. I wanted so bad to hug him and feel his body in my arms one more time. Damn, I missed him. There was so much I wanted to share and express to him. I wanted to prolong this visit for as long as I could.

"That's their fight, dude. Whatever makes them happy," he said waving his hand in the air.

"What happened?" I asked.

"You really want me to tell you?" he chuckled, looking at me like really nigga?

"Yeah, I asked, right?" I smiled.

"My dad cheated," he said.

"Damn, I'm sorry about that," I said feeling slightly awkward.

"Well, a man is going to be a man and do what he wants according to my dad," Jason said shrugging his shoulders.

"Was it on camera?" I joked.

"No! You punk! That's your area of expertise," he said. He reached over and ripped a grape from the vine and threw it at me.

"Jason, I'm joking," I said.

"Oh yeah, well find an appropriate subject to joke about!" he said sucking his teeth and folding his arms again. He had his guard up for most of this visit. I was trying to get him to lighten up a little.

"Yo', I apologize, babes. All jokes aside though, Jason. I'm sorry about what happened between us. If I could do things differently, God knows I fuckin' would," I said.

"Gary, what happened has happened, okay? I'm over it," he said. His abrupt tone stung.

"Damn, like that?" I asked.

"What you mean? Like what?" he smirked and shrugged his shoulders.

"I'm over it!" I said mocking him. "Why you gotta say it like that, Jason?"

"Gary, I mean what am I supposed to say, oh thank you so much for giving me Syphilis. Hell, I still have one more shot to take next week before I can really feel like a normal man again. I just got that voicemail message today. I mean, do you realize just how messed up in the head I am over this crap. You got me scared to get close to anybody else. You and your ex gave me a really nice parting gift, so yes, I'm over it!" he boldly stated clearing the air.

"Jason, I fucked up and I own up to it. I'm not perfect. I have a problem, but I'm ready to change," I said.

"I hear you talking," he said.

"Are you over me? I asked hesitantly. I was hoping his answer would be no.

"Look, I'll be there for you when you need me and I'm going to leave it at that. We've already discussed that Gary. Let's just let the past be the past. I came to check on you and make sure you were okay. That's it," he said grabbing the bedside rail. My instincts were telling me that there was more to this visit.

"Well, I'm glad you came. I missed you," I said seizing the opportunity to caress his hand lightly. I could see him tense up. His skin felt so smooth, and the energy radiating from that contact reminded me that much more of how good he felt in my hands.

"Cool. I'm glad you're getting better," he said. There was a moment of awkward silence that filled the room. I wondered what was going through his head as my hand covered his. The fact that he didn't retreat gave me just the glimmer of hope I needed.

"For real, Jay, do you miss me?" I asked before being interrupted by Moms.

"Jason, is that you, cutie pie?" Moms asked. Jason snatched his hand away from under my very own. Moms sat a big thermo bag down in a chair next to the bed, walked up behind Jason, and placed a hand on his shoulder squeezing it. Jason turned around to give her a warm hug. She was extremely delighted to see him and was all smiles as they swayed side to side. I took this opportunity to peek at that booty again.

"Yes, ma'am, the one and only," Jason said glancing at his watch.

"Ooooh, how I missed those dimples. Look at that handsome fellow, Gary. See what you missing out on?" Moms said making him blush. She was clinging on to him. Jason stood there looking bashful and unsure of what to do with himself as she kissed him on the cheek.

"Mama, what brings you by?" I asked. As happy as I was to see her, I was still trying to get to the bottom of Jason's feelings towards me.

"Sorry to disturb you two. I just felt a need to stop by and bring you some Conch Chowder and Johnny Cakes. I wanted to eat with my oldest boy since you couldn't make it to the house tonight for dinner," Moms said leaning in to kiss me on my cheek. "Jason, you one lucky boy, I got just enough for you too. So stop looking at that watch of yours. You're not going anyplace," she smiled kissing him on the cheek and hugging his again.

"Yes, ma'am. I'll stay for a minute," Jason said.

"Good, now can you do me two favors, boy?" Moms asked, letting her accent take over. "Yes, I can," he answered.

"Stop calling me ma'am. It's Momma. You know who I am, right?" Moms said looking him in the eye. She put her hands on her hips waiting for him to say the right answer.

"Yes, Momma. I remember," he said winking his eye at me.

"That's better. Now the second thing I need you to do is help Gary out of bed, so you two can go wash your hands while I prepare this good food," she said moving over to her bag. Jason removed his jacket and hoodie and did as she asked. It felt good as fuck having two of my favorite people in the whole wide world to share my favorite meal with me that evening. Jason still was on my radar and though we still had much to talk about, I had a feeling that it was going to be alright. Moms being there confirmed that for me.

Visitation Rights...

"So have you fucked Javi yet? Excuse me, has Javi fucked you?" Michael asked clearing his throat.

"No, but we've lightly messed around. I want to chill on the sex tip and wait until I'm sure I want to be with him. Now what he did tell me was that once that door is open, he has a high sex drive," I said. I had to keep up the appearance of Javi and me until I was ready to tell them what happened.

"Jason, clarification needed. What the hell is lightly messing around?" Preston asked before Michael interjected.

"Chile, that boy fucking. You just don't know about it." Michael said.

"Shut up and do your set," I said smiling handing him a 40 lbs. dumbbell.

"I'm telling you. As phyne as that boy is!" Michael said.

"I know right. Well, we went and got tested a couple days ago and if the results come back negative, then I might consider it," I lied. I hadn't planned on having sex with anyone just yet.

"Jason, is he uncut? I know you've seen it," Preston said.

"Yeah, I've only seen it because he took a shower at my house," I said finishing a set of crunches on an activity ball. There was a moment of silence in our vicinity. Michael and Preston were both staring at me when I turned around to finally make eye contact with them. I was startled slightly.

"Well?" Michael said. "What?" I said smiling.

"Oh, Jason, don't play coy with us sweetie. Answer the question," Preston said.

"He's uncut," I said in a quiet voice.

"Ewww. Banana with cheese. I knew it!" Michael said. He and Preston burst into laughter and slapped one another high five.

"Ha, ha, ha! Dudes that are uncut are normally extra sensitive in that area. It's hot to me," I said shrugging my shoulders.

"Latino, the other white meat," Preston expressed with thumbs up as we all laughed again.

"Hell, Gary was uncut," I said slapping him a high five.

"I couldn't do it," Michael said. He sat on the ball to do a set of crunches. "It's like a ummm...a turtle head popping in and out of its shell," he stated. He had this look on his face like something in the room stunk.

"Michael. Really? Some of the boys you've messed with? Really?" I said.

"Okay! Chile, you've no room to talk about what's nasty! We've witnessed many of the trashy little thirsty versatile tragic power bottoms you've slayed over the years," Preston scoffed. He then let out a quick laugh.

"In your professional opinion, do you think there are any other words needed to describe your bust downs?" I asked being blatantly sarcastic.

"Yeah, he did, with big tight clean booties. The rest is whatever," Michael said.

"Yeah. About that," I said chuckling at his comment. I dabbed the sweat from my forehead with the lime green gym towel in my hand.

"Well. Make sure he cleans his dick really well before you stick it in your mouth. I can just imagine lint, sweat, and piss droplets being trapped in that skin," Michael said. He licked his tongue out and contorted his face as if he had just bit into a lemon.

"Okay, let's get off his dick, freak nasty. Enough is enough. The point is," I paused for dramatic effect. "I'm not rushing into bed with anybody right now. I don't even know if I want to go there for real for real. I'm just talking out loud," I said dabbing my forehead with the gym towel again.

"You two do look cute together. I do approve. I couldn't see it at first until I saw you guys at the party," Preston said, stretching his calf muscles.

"I like him a lot. I'm just taking it light," I said.

"Hag! Let that boy get that hole," Michael said.

He stood up and started humping the air and pretending he was smacking a booty.

"In due time big bro!" I said stretching my arms.

"Okay, so my next question comes in the form of Darius," Preston said batting his eyelashes. I smiled thinking how to address the question. "I haven't really thought about... I'm lying," I said laughing.

"I know you are, hag!" Preston said smiling.

"No, I mean, that's probably the reason I'm hesitating," I lied. Gary was becoming the reason. "But yo, I mean Javi is here," I said. I was hoping to gain some type of clarity soon as to what to do. It was as if I was on a game show with three different doors from which to choose.

"And he's phyne as hell," Preston said taking a sip of water.

"Yes, he is phyne!" I said gushing. "It's really a no-brainer, right?"

"Puerto Rican papi, used to be a deacon, now he be suckin' me off on the weekend!" Preston and I said quoting female rapper Lil' Kim. We slapped one another a high five. We would always break out into some Lil' Kim verse at the same time as if we shared one brain.

"This ho and these pretty boys. See that's your problem. You always end up falling for Rover the Red Bone Dog," Michael said shaking his head.

"What are you talking about? I do not. And furthermore, Michael, you are light bright and do the same freakin' thing!" I said.

"Indeed, but this is a conversation about Jason Williams, not Michael Cox. I like my men dark," he said slyly as I rolled my eyes and smiled. "You always fall for the pretty boy type with the light eyes and light skin. The fools who ain't gon' do nothing but dog you out in the end."

"Umm, the Michaels of the world?" Preston chimed in and gave him a cute little wave and cheesy grin.

"Okay, guys like me, I can admit that. The quintessential player who has a hundred fuckin' bottoms pushing up on them," Michael said.

"Javi ain't like that though," I said. We returned the lose equipment we were working with and walked over to the treadmills.

"Neither was Gary," Michael said. He threw his arm around me and drew me in closer to him. I felt myself wanting to defend Gary, but resisted the urge.

"Ooop! He has a point, sweetie," Preston said biting his finger.

"Really Preston? You just gon' cosign like that?" I asked sarcastically. "Okay, hags, any man can be a dog," I said.

"Yeah, but these pretty faced men go through life getting everything handed to them. They shit on everybody because they think they can. And to add insult to injury, people let them. I should know. I don't want to see that happen to you again. How do you know Javier ain't a dog?" Michael asked.

"That's the beauty of it. I don't know. And for the record, I don't only go for one type of dude," I said stepping up onto a treadmill.

"Jason. You could be dick-mitized right now. It happens to the best of us. You know how you get. You believe everything a man tells you versus what he shows you," Preston said. I looked over at him with my mouth agape gagging.

"Yes! My point exactly! You summed that up rather nicely Preston," Michael said. Preston nodded sipping some water.

"You'd better read me, Preston," I laughed shaking my head.

"Seriously. I warned you about Gary. It was just something too good to be true about his arrogant ass. And you probably still contemplating getting back with him, huh?" Michael said with a smirk.

"For real, I'm good on Gary, okay?" I lied again wondering if I was becoming transparent in reference to my internal conflict. I also wanted to address the little "arrogant" comment Mike made in reference to Gary, but again, I chose not to address the bashing.

"All I'm saying is be careful this   time," Michael said.

"Well, Michael, do you suspect anything from Javi?" I asked. We all started jogging.

"We're going to start on 7.0 for speed with a two percent incline fellas," Preston said. I increased my incline and grabbed my towel.

"Hmmm. Honestly. I think Darius is a keeper. Don't play him to the left just yet. I really think he'd be good for you. Now I'm saying this as a friend. We're in the truth tree right now. Javi is cool, I don't know, Jason. It's some tea there. Plus, he's still a pretty boy. It's too early for me to make an assessment. I'll get back to you on him," Michael said.

"You know what you have a vendetta against other fair skinned kats," I said laughing.

"Not really. I treat all booties equal, but I am team dark skin at the end of the day," Michael said winking his eye at me. "Hell, you could have been my prey," he said reaching over to touch me.

"You know what I wish we were having this conversation on the phone, so I could push end," I said shaking my head and motioning away from his reach. "Don't touch me."

"You knew he was going to revert back to sex," Preston laughed.

"I know right! Captain cave top, the slut bag, over here!" I said pointing.

"And clearly, he secretly wants to be dark skinned," Preston whispered. I smiled nodding my head in agreement.

"My God, my God, look at him. See, God ain't right. He was not fair when he created the black man. We got it all. Brains, booties, thighs, thick lips, and good dick. Goodness gracious bring that ass back!" Michael said looking in the mirror observing one of the patrons walking by.

"Yes sir, he is phyne!" I said. "He has that cute boy on the basketball team look happening," I said illustrating my point.

"I'm hitting that tonight. Um hmm, sure am," Michael said making eye contact with the guy as he walked back. He smiled and gave Michael the nod.

"I'm sure you are. Is it that easy?" Preston said rolling his eyes.

"For Michael, I hate to admit, it really is just that easy," I smiled and winked at Michael. "He's irresistibly cute, with his mannish butt."

"You know, Jason, it's his insidious aggressive sexual approach with any of these guys, that lets them know he just wants to play butt darts," Preston said as I laughed. "What about him Mike?" Preston said inconspicuously pointing at a random guy on an elliptical machine.

"I fucked him last week," Michael said glancing in the direction Preston was pointing in. "His asshole is wide as a coffee can. He's ruined. I had to dial up one of my regular bust downs to finish what shawty started." Michael chuckled. Preston rolled his eyes and looked over at me.

"You asked Preston," I said laughing. I dabbed my face with my towel. "I thought he was straight?" I said looking over at Michael surprised that my gaydar failed me.

"Jason in life you learn that straight boys in mirrors are gayer than they appear," he said throwing up a peace sign at a guy walking by who gave us a head nod.

"Shouldn't one be somewhat pedantic when it comes to sex? I mean, it's the difference between the chase and being romantic, versus getting ate out and screwed in some random bathroom stall at 24 Hour Fitness," I said.

"That's the beauty of sex between men. It can go down anyplace at any time. See dude over there?" Michael said motioning to a guy sipping water at the fountain. Preston and I looked over in that direction as Michael continued his story. "I hit that in the sauna late one night. Shawty was on some games at first, acting all scary, talking about how he just wanted to suck my dick. I was like, if I pull my dick out, you pulling that ass out. Head just ain't gon' cut it. So you either getting fucked, or I'm leaving. So finally, I get him in the steam room, he do what he do sucking my dick, and then I bent him over, put it where his ribs is at, cleaned up the dick, and dipped out."

"Meet, beat, and skeet," I said.

"That's the way it goes, baby!" Michael smiled.

"Speaking of that, can you tell your boy with the bad teeth to lose my number," Preston said referring to one of the guys Michael works with. One night at the club, Preston gave the boy his number because he was looking at him through beer goggles. The next day the guy sent his picture, and I mean he was cute for somebody, but not my boy Preston. Plus, the guy really needed to see an Orthodontist.

"Aww, Preston, I was just trying to turn you on to some good dick. The boys say he has a serious stroke game that almost rivals mine of course." Michael boasted proudly.

"Really?!" I blurted out.

"Plus he brushes and flosses," Michael said turning towards me with a wink.

"With what? Rope!" I quickly interjected; we all shared a quick laugh.

"You bitches are so choosey. Okay. I have a question," Michael said.

"Oh God, what another top bottom thing?" Preston asked smiling.

"No, I want to know if Shawn is going to be here for Thanksgiving?" Michael asked.

"From what he tells me, he's going home. He wants to introduce Andre to Mrs. Winnie B. I am so jealous. I wish I could bring my boyfriend home for the holidays," I said.

"Chile, I wish I had someone worth bringing home," Preston said.

"You still not going home?" Michael asked me.

"I'm not thinking about my folks this year. I think my mama is going to Detroit to visit. Me and my dad aren't really speaking and I just want to chill with my dog," I said nonchalantly.

"Good, well, you can make the dressing. Preston said he's staying too," Michael said.

"You are?" I asked looking over at him.

"Yeah, my parents are going on a cruise, but I'm going home for Christmas though. I'm going to redeem that ticket from spring break that I didn't get to use," Preston said.

"Okay cool, we can have dinner at my crib then. Ya'll can invite Gary, I mean..." I said pausing in mid-sentence. I shut my eyes and laughed at myself.

"Wow. Why is that boy all up and through your spirit?" Michael said giving me the side eye. I avoided making direct eye contact with him.

"Yeah, we'll invite, Gary, Jason, and you can invite Javi over for dinner. Deal?" Preston said looking at me in the mirror smiling.

"Ya'll knew what I meant," I said.

"Speaking of dates, you better hope Darius don't get an R & R from Kuwait for the holidays," Michael said.

"I know, I'm going to have to eventually tell him about the situation, but we aren't together. And I think it would be best to wait until he returns to tell him news like that. That is the wrong environment to dish that kind of tea," I said.

"Umm hmm," Michael said.

"You know what I mean. You're still in the Navy. You don't want to get bad news on a deployment," I said. I looked down at the console on the treadmill to see how long we had been running.

"You're right. I'm just messing with you, but you need to handle that. I think Darius is the truth and he gon' smell another nigga's piss. You know real tops are territorial," he warned.

"Perhaps. I don't know," I said. I looked away picking up my towel and wrapped it around my fist.

"Yeah you do. Like I said, that's why you're not ready to let Javi poke you," Michael said.

"I guess. But the crazy thing is I haven't heard from Darius in a minute." My thoughts flashed back to the last phone conversation we had. I hoped there weren't extenuating circumstances that caused him to have to hang up so abruptly. He was in a war zone, and I tried not to think the worst of things when it came to him being over there, but being a former military man myself, you know that things can change and happen at a moment's notice.

"Really?" Preston asked.

"Yeah. I hope everything is alright," I said.

"Well, don't think the worst, sweetie. I'm sure he has a lot going on over there." Preston said attempting to put any negative thoughts to rest.

"Yeah, you're right. I'm probably being paranoid," I smiled and glanced at him in the mirror.

We finished our run and parted ways for the evening. We were going to get together at Michael's place for Top Model later in the week. As normal I had to rush home to walk Batman. I sort of forgot about him today and I hoped he didn't make a mess out of the bathroom. I couldn't blame him if he did though. Every once in a while he'll throw a little temper tantrum if I steer too far off of the schedule I tried to keep for him.

I pulled into my garage and hurried to Batman who was whimpering in the bathroom. I opened the door and he darted out running towards the front entrance. I grabbed his doggy harness, and opened the door to let him out. He ran down the porch stairs and relieved himself on the front lawn. He ran back up to me and greeted me excitedly.

"You are such a silly little doggy. I'm sorry, batty boy. I'm sorry. Come on. You want to go for a walk? Huh? You want a walk?" I said as I snapped the harness around his little body. He was licking my hands and steadied himself as I strapped him up, walked him, and took a shower before starting my reading assignment. I placed my phone on the charger, took a deep breath and opened the book to chapter 12. I didn't feel like reading, but it was something that had to be done. So that I wouldn't get distracted I kept the music off. But wouldn't you know it, as soon as I got comfortable and good into the chapter, my phone rang. It was my mom. I grabbed my blue tooth and pressed the button to answer the call.

"Mother, what a pleasant surprise," I smiled joking with her.

"Hey boy. What are you doing?" she asked.

"Sitting here trying to get some homework done. I just got in not too long ago," I said.

"Oh yeah?" She said.

"Yup, what's up? You doing okay?" I asked. I was going to attempt to speed this conversation up so that I could get back to my studies. I was anticipating the same dry questions I usually received from my folks, especially since the holidays were upon us.

"I'm good. Listen, what are you doing for Thanksgiving?" she asked.

"I was just going to stay here. My friends and I are going to get together and cook and hang out. Nothing major this year," I said. I really didn't want to go home for the holidays. I assumed she was going to ask me to do so with everything going on with her and Dad.

"Well, I was going to come up there and see you," Mama said. I put the book down, and shuffled to sit on the edge of the bed. I took the blue tooth off, and grabbed the phone. Batman ran over to investigate my quick action. I picked him up and placed him on the bed.

"What do you mean? You're coming to see me?" I asked out of confusion and curiosity. I had been asking this woman for years to come and visit me at the various duty stations I was assigned to, all to no avail. Especially Chicago, since she had always talked about wanting to go on the Oprah Winfrey show. Never once did she ever volunteer to come and see me, her only son. I was curious to know if I was being Punk'd because this was definitely out of the ordinary.

"What? I need visitation rights to come see my child?"

"Naw, nothing like that. It's just a shock," I said scratching my head. I couldn't believe my ears. She actually wanted to come and see me in my own personal space. I was elated but hesitant about getting my hopes up. For years I had witnessed my friends' mothers and fathers making special trips to visit them, and it was a pleasure meeting them. Admittedly, I was envious at them because of it. I felt like I would never have that experience, so a part of me was letting that dream die slowly, but thank God for faith.

"Listen. I've been doing a lot of thinking about what you said. And I would like to get to know my son. You were right about what you said to me when you were here. It hurt to hear, but it hurt more knowing that you felt that way, and that I was doing that to you," she said.

"I don't know what to say," I said. I was overcome with emotion at that point. I could barely breathe. I didn't know whether to cry, scream in sheer delight, or laugh nervously out loud to express the excitement doing flips within me. I was trembling.

"You already said enough. I lost my husband... but I don't want to lose my kids. So I want to come and get to know you and visit with you and your friends and start fresh," Mama said.

"Okay. Well, I am... wow! Ma, I am happy to hear that." I paused to contain myself. The logical side of me wanted to play it cool. "When are you coming so I can take some more time off? I only took the day before the holiday off, so I have to adjust my patient load. So let me know what days you are interested in coming," I said.

"I was looking at that Tuesday through the weekend," she said.

"Okay, I will go ahead and put my leave in for that week," I said.

"Well that's all I wanted," she said.

"Okay," I smiled. I was still in shock.

Visitation Rights... "Alright boy, I'll talk to you later.

"Okay. Um... Mama?" I said.

"What?" she said.

"Thank you. I love you," I said.

"I love you too," she said. It was the first time in my adult life that I had heard her speak those words with a meaningful and heartfelt tone. It wasn't forced, rushed, or rehearsed. It felt genuine this time. All of the praying I did allowed me to look at faith in a whole new light. I looked up towards the sky and whispered a thank you to God. A tear rolled down my cheek as I lay back on the bed. If this relationship was being strengthened, what was next?

Back in Love Again...

I was waiting for Jason to come around with the car. Jason had agreed to pick me up and take me to today's physical therapy appointment since it was one of his off days. I didn't feel like driving and had worked the shit out of my leg and back today, so it was good that I hadn't drove. The CNA and I were shooting the breeze about the dramatic temperature drop when Jason pulled up and opened the passenger door. I told the young lady that this was my ride, and she wheeled me out to the car. The cold air, hit me like a ton of bricks. I got out of the chair and the girl assisted me into the car. Jason took my bag and put in it in the trunk. She closed the door and waved goodbye. I waved back. Jason got in and closed his door.

"Jay, turn the heat on, babes!" I said rubbing my hands together.

"I was trying to let the car warm up a little bit. It ain't gon' do nothing but blow cold air on you," he said adjusting the thermostat.

"It should be good now. See?" I said holding my hands out over the vents.

"So how are you? You feel one hundred?" he said looking at me and smiling.

"Well, I'm better than can be expected. For the doctor wanting me to take it easy on my knee, that session was no punk! Non strenuous activity my ass," I said adjusting my seat back.

"Well, you make sure you are taking it easy outside of your sessions. Don't be the tough guy. You know how you do," Jason said lecturing me like he used too.

"What you mean by that?"

"Oh so now you gon' act? You remember that time you got stung by that wasp and blew up like a freakin' circus balloon...talking about, I don't need to see no doctor. I'm cool," he mocked me and started laughing afterwards.

"Man, I was good. It would have passed. Shit, it was just a little swelling," I said grinning.

"Yeah. An allergic reaction constricting your airway constitutes more than swelling dude. You keep on being the tough guy if you want too?" Jason warned. I felt the warmth in his smile today. It got me thinking.

"That's what attracted you to me though," I said placing my arm around his seat. I gripped the headrest with my hand. I wanted to caress the nape of his neck like old times, but I needed to be subtle in my approach.

"So you were being hard for me?" he asked ambiguously. He looked over at me and smiled.

"Hell yeah! I had to man up! Letting you know yo' man ain't no punk!" I said flexing my biceps.

"Here you go! This is not a Geico commercial caveman," he laughed.

"So what's new with you?" I asked.

"Nothing. Oh, guess who's coming to visit me for turkey day?" Jason asked glancing over at me. He did a little cute bounce.

"Me?" I said.

"Nope! Not this year," he said laughing hysterically.

"Old mean ass! Who's coming to dinner then?" I said sticking my tongue out at him.

"My mama. YAY!" he said. He was beaming with joy as he shared his good news with me.

"Oh get the fuck out of here. That's what's up! You sound happy about it?" I said tapping his arm.

"Uh huh. She says that she wants to meet my friends, and see my new place, and all that good junk. She wants to get to know Jason, the adult. I am so excited, Gary!" I loved to see him when he was bubbly and excited. He had the sexiest little can't sit still boyish charm.

"What brought about this change of heart?" I asked. I knew how much Jason wanted his family to accept and love him for who he was. It was great that his mom was coming around. I knew her taking time to come and visit him would mean the world to him. I had witnessed the hurt they inflicted on him time and time again because they didn't agree with his lifestyle as they put it. I remember calling his moms phone one day and getting voicemail. I wanted to tell her about herself and that she was missing out on the best thing that ever happened to me. I debated on going off on her voicemail, but hung up instead. Jason had no clue that I had made the call to her. That's how much I care about him.

"Well, I had a long talk with her the last time I was home. I put it all on the table about how they don't know me, and that I would like to include them in my life more, but they shut me out so much because of this fear of what they think gay people are or represent," he said.

"So she obviously listened to you?" I said.

"Obviously. She told me she doesn't want to lose her children. I'm looking forward to this. I told Mike and them, and they are like, yes, we have to see where the hell you came from," he paused and laughed. "So they'll all be here except for Shawn. I am glad this is happening," Jason said.

"When will she be in town?" I asked.

"She'll be here Tuesday, the 20th," he said with a big Kool Aide smile.

"Thanksgiving is when?"

"It's the 22nd this year."

"You ready?" I asked.

"Yeah. I wish I could clone myself because it is so much I have to do between now and then. I want this to be perfect, you know," he glanced over at me. "It's like I'm starting over with her. I don't know," he laughed.

"Yeah, pace yourself there, buddy. It's going to be fine," I said. He was like a kid at Christmas. He looked so cute and I just wanted to eat him up because I missed moments like this with Jason. I wish I could have been there by his side the night he got the call from his mom. I also wished I could be the one by his side when she arrived. It would have been a pleasure to meet my mother-in-law in our old home.

"You think so?" Jason asked sounding a little unsure.

"Of course it will. You know how anal you are about everything," I laughed.

"Forget you, punk. I'm thorough!" he said.

"Which is pretty much another word for...?" I said giving the come on hand gesture.

"Whatever dude!" he laughed slapping my good leg.

He was on cloud nine about this news. I knew how important this was to him. He was somewhat envious of the relationship I had with my parents. They not only knew my sexuality but also accepted it and loved me unconditionally. He never really showed it, but I knew there was that void in his life. He always tried to hide his vulnerability, even around me at times. We pulled in front of my crib and Jason helped me inside my apartment.

"Don't let me fall," I joked.

"I got you, come on old man," Jason said laughing supporting me on my left side.

"They shoulda' gave me a set of crutches, shit!" I said.

"Gary, you don't need crutches. You aren't supposed to be babying your knee," he said helping me up the stairs. We walked up to my apartment and he grabbed my keys to open the door.

"Now don't be raggin' on my crib now," I said realizing that it wouldn't be up to his standards of cleanliness.

"I wasn't going to say nothing," he said shaking his head.

"Yeah, but I know what's going through your head. Ol' Obsessive Compulsive Disorder havin' ass," I laughed.

"Wow. It is cleaner than I expected though," he said taking a survey of the living room. He placed my bag down and sat on the couch.

"You want some water or something to drink?" I asked walking into the kitchen.

"No I'm good," he said.

"Well, I do. I got to take these damn pills," I said walking out of the kitchen into the living room. I crashed on the couch and opened a pill bottle. I took a Motrin out, popped it into my mouth, and chased it with a gulp of water.

"You want this bag in your room?" Jason asked. He now had his hands in his pocket and was leaning up against the wall.

"Oh hell yeah! Are you hinting at something?" I smiled. I winked at his lil' sexy ass.

"Negro please! I'm just trying to be a good steward," he said sucking his teeth.

"Um huh. I need to go back there anyway. Follow me sir," I said slowly standing up. I winced as I put weight on my left leg.

"Are you okay?" Jason asked bending down to grab my bag.

"Yeah. It's just uncomfortable to pivot. My back is a little sore," I said. He followed me down the hallway.

"Poor thing," he said rubbing my lower back. I was milking the attention just a little bit.

"I know, right?"

"I like these floors. You got a cool lil' spot," he said looking at a painting I had on the wall.

"I'm glad you like it, but I want to see your crib though," I said.

"We'll see about that," he said sitting the bag down. I plopped down on the bed and started stretching out my leg.

"This shit is for the birds Jay. Oh my God."

"I know it is. Just keep doing the stretches and take your medicine. It's going to get better, I promise," he said offering comfort.

"I know but this shit hurt babes," I said pouting.

"Take one of the Vicodin and lay down. Do   you have any juice?" he asked.

"I have some grape juice in the frig. Damn, this ain't cool," I chuckled.

"Take it easy with all that bending. You need to be easy on your back too Gary," he said helping me with the pillows.

"Thank you," I smiled taking in the fragrant cologne he was wearing.

"Remember pain is nothing but weakness leaving the body," Jason smiled.

"I'ma fuck you up," I said with a dismissive look. He unlaced and removed my shoes and folded a pillow in half placing it under my knee with great care.

"Alright, chill here. I'll be right back," Jason said handing me the remote. I turned the T.V. on. He came back a few minutes later with a couple of toasted ham and cheese sandwiches, a bag of chips, an apple cut into fourths, juice, and my pills.

"Oh snap, look at you taking care of me. Thank you, Jay!" I said.

"Well, you don't want to take these meds with nothing on your stomach, especially Vicodin. Trust me I know," he said handing me the plate of food.

"Cool," I said. I grabbed one of the sandwiches and took a huge bite out of it.

"Gary! Oh my God, how did you hide this from me? I haven't seen this trophy in so long," he said pulling the small gold plated trophy out of a box I had tucked away in the corner. There was a picture stuffed inside of it. He eyed the trophy and pulled the picture from the cup.

"Oh shit. I remember that thing," I laughed. We had won it at an LGBT stepper set dinner cruise.

"I remember that night. That was the first true Chicago thing I did. Learning how to step. I was concentrating hard as hell so that I wouldn't step on your toes."

"You did a great job though babes," I said giving him a wink.

"I had a great teacher," he smiled. He glanced over at me. I noticed he bit his lower lip before studying the picture again. He seemed to be strolling down memory lane.

"No doubt!" I smiled. I finished the last bit of one sandwich.

"We looked good didn't we?" Jason said handing me the picture.

"Yup! We did, huh?" I said wiping my hands. I took a look at the picture.

"You couldn't tell us nothing that night," Jason said gleaming with pride.

"Look at that smile. I miss that," I said looking up at him.

"Cool," he said avoiding eye contact with me.

"I miss you," I said.

"I miss you too. Kind of," he said hesitantly. He was still avoiding eye contact with me.

"Why are you scared to look at me all of a sudden?" I asked. I sat the plate down and slid towards the foot of the bed. Jason was leaning on my dresser.

"I'm not... I'm just..." he paused placing the trophy down on the dresser.

"What's up? What you doing then?" I said pulling him closer to me. He gripped my forearms with a little resistance and inhaled deeply with his eyes closed.

"I'm just reminiscing. That's all," he said. He finally opened his eyes and I was able to see the depth of their beauty up close and personal again. They captured the light with such clarity revealing a deep brown that was unmistakably the hue God intended when He spoke that pigment into existence.

"You miss me?" I asked resting my head in his chest. He smelled so fuckin' good. I could feel his body tense as I squeezed his frame.

"Yeah I do," he said in a quiet shaky voice.

"I don't know what happened, babes. But I'm sorry for it all. You just don't know," I said.

"It's the past, Gary. It's done, okay?" Jason said trying to free himself from my grip. I couldn't let him go. Hell, I didn't want to let him go. I needed him to understand. I needed him to forgive me. I needed for him to come back to me. I needed to be intimate with him again. I needed him to feel my love for him reinforced sexually with me deep inside of his body.

"I hate my fucking self for hurting you and passing that shit on to you," I confessed being brutally honest. "I took so much from you by thinking with my dick. I never want to hurt you again baby. I promise I won't. I need you. I miss what we had, Jason."

"I know. I miss it too, but things..." Jason said.

"Are different. I know." I interrupted.

"Well hey, um... I need to go, I will..."

"Um mmm. Shhhh. Hold on! Let me just enjoy holding you for a few minutes. Shhhh!" I said squeezing his body tighter. He didn't say anything. He just put   his arms around me and let me hold him as I demanded. I stood up still holding on to him. I kissed his forehead and then slowly moved in to kiss his lips gently. He pushed away before I could make contact with them.

"Gary, I should go. I can't do this with you, it's too confusing," he said. He hit me in my chest with his fist trying to break away from me. I understood why he hit me. I didn't care. I held my ground.

"I'm sorry. I just miss you," I said kissing his forehead again. I held on to him tighter so he couldn't run away from me. He hit me in the chest again two more times. I took his blows but would not let go.

I felt like if I kissed him, it would rekindle what we had. I ran my hands down his back sliding them individually into his jean pockets. I had a firm grip on him as he made another attempt to push away. I eased my way to his lips and made contact. I opened my eyes and realized that his were closed. He was frozen breathing rapidly and unsure of what to do. I took the lead and parted his lips with my tongue. He kissed me back, still tensed up, but enjoying the presence of me there. I knew him all too well. He was eventually going to give in and open up to me. I felt him caress my face ever so gently as our lips parted ways. I continued holding on to him. I opened my eyes again and he followed suit. A tear ran down his left cheek. I caught it with a kiss asking him what was wrong.

"Why are you fighting so hard for me?" He asked. He was still in a frozen state of tense anxiety as his eyes pierced through mine. He had his guard up trying to figure out if this was a feckless attempt at getting some ass.

"Jason, I'm going to sound real cliché right now," I paused rubbing his back trying to get him to loosen up and trust me again. I was so nervous because I knew I had to address this moment with some delicacy. I said what I had wanted to say to him for so many months now. "I love you. You're more than worth the fight, baby. I'm hopelessly in love with you, Jason," I said kissing his lips yet again.

"I thought the world of you Gary," he said as a new tear made its way down his left cheek. I wiped it away with my thumb and took a deep breath still clinging to him.

"Please say you still love me, babes, I need you in my life. Don't be afraid of me," I pleaded. He sighed looking up towards the ceiling with his eyes closed before looking back at me.

"I really don't want to tell you anything, Gary. I'm hurt and I'm pissed at you," he jabbed my chest again, letting his emotions flow. I stood there clinging to his frame as he let loose. "You had the nerve to lay next to me like nothing ever happened, then ask me if I'm happy being with you, or what did you say... did I ever think about being with other dudes. Well, guess what, Gary? I got lost in you. You were supposed to be the one to protect me and offer me a place of rest. Do you know how good it felt to be able to rely on someone other than myself, huh?" he said waiting for me to respond.

"I can only imagine, babes," I said listening to him.

"I've been doing this thing on my own for years, Gary. My family hates me and my friends can only be so much to me. I have two other wonderful guys at my beckoning call right now, dude, and I'm sitting here pissed and pining over what was once the most important thing in the world to me. With you, it was supposed to be all right. It was supposed to be okay. I'm scared to get caught up like that again. But..." he said catching his breath and looking away from me.

"Talk to me, babes, please let it all out. I know I fucked up, I'm not perfect, I cheat because I'm selfish, Jason. I want what I can't have and I have... no... had what I don't deserve, but I swear to you baby, if you give me another chance, I'm going to earn your trust, you, and your heart," I still had a hold on him as he began to vent again.

"You got any other exes you trying to screw? Because I promise if you cheat on me again I'm going to do more than exit dramatically," he said with a seriousness in his face that was new to me.

"I promise my past is behind me, Jason. You're my focus," I said as he took a minute to study my face. I was anxious as to what would happen next as I prayed God would give me back my man.

"Gary, when I got that call from your sister, all I could think about was holding you and hoping that I'd get another opportunity to see you. I realized just how much I missed you," he said.

"Say that you love me still. Please, Jason," I begged.

"If you were to turn me inside out, you'd see that I can't help but love you. I forgive you," he said with more tears following the previous two. "I'm still in love with you," he said finally letting go of the tension holding him back from me. I was overcome with emotion hearing these words come from his quivering full lips. It was also the first time I had seen him shed tears.

He locked his hands around my neck and placed a kiss on my lips so full of passion. I finally got my man back. I scooped him up and pulled him on top of me parting his legs so that he could comfortably straddle me. We looked into each other's eyes as if time were standing still. I was glad to know that the passion between us was still there as we repeatedly professed and confirmed our love for one another. I vowed never to stray away from him again. We kissed slowly for hours exchanging and releasing old feelings, past hurt, and rebuilding what was meant to be.

For the first time, my heart and mind agreed to take a chance together. Jason was back in my life. I had dealt with my issues, and had been forgiven by the man of my dreams. Haley's Comet had nothing on him. Jason ended up spending the night with me and we lay in each other's arms kissing, napping, catching up, and getting to know the men that we'd become in the time that passed between us. I kept waking up and smiling realizing that I wasn't dreaming. We were a reality again. At some point through the night, I noticed he was missing. I jumped up and went to search for him. I breathe a sigh of relief and I saw he was on my computer pecking away at the keys. I walked up behind him relieved that he hadn't left. He was wearing a pair of my sweat pants and the light from the desk lamp reflected off of his smooth bare chest.

"What's up, Mr. Larrieux?" he said smiling looking up at me. I moved my head down close to his face as if I were going to kiss him.

"Hot Cheetos breath," I whispered, making sure he got a whiff of my breath.

"Back up off me! Ol' nasty bastard!" he said laughing and pushing me away. I burst into laughter.

"Damn, why I gotta be all that?" I said still laughing.

"Because you're disgusting," he said getting up from the chair. He walked up to me and kissed my lips sweetly.

"Babes, you should have seen your face! That shit was priceless," I said. He wrapped his arms around my neck and I gripped his waist.

"Ha! Ha! Ha!" he said.

"What you in here doing, and how long is it going to take you to finish? I need some lovin'," I said.

"I had to pull my assignment from my email and edit it a little bit so I can turn it in on time. I'm not going to be too much longer, boo, I promise. You just go and brush your teeth," he said. I gave his lips a peck.

"How long?" I said biting his ear and rubbing his head.

"Give me 15 minutes," Jason said.

"Just fifteen?" I said.

"Fifteen minutes. Tops."

"Yeah, that's what I'ma be doing. Toppin'!" I said pointing to myself. "Don't make me come back in here and get you," I said as I rubbed his head again.

"You threatening me now?"

"I'm threatening to beat that shit up on this computer desk if you not in the bed with me in 15 minutes," I said biting his neck. He reached into my shorts and grabbed my dick.

"Is this what you're threatening me with?" He was smiling seductively and bit his lip. That shit turned me the fuck on.

"Uh huh, I'm trying to put that dick all up in you," I said. He stood on his tip toes and kissed his way to my ear.

"You lost that privilege. And when you do get it back, you're on condom detail buddy," Jason said. He stood back and patted me on the shoulder.

"Damn, babes, I promise I'm clean, and I know you are. We're good, you just gon' leave me here on brick?" I smiled. He winked and nodded his head yes.

"Umm, I wasn't easy the first time, and I won't be easy this time," he said folding his arms. I had to respect that.

"Jason."

"What, Gary?" he smirked.

"You ain't let no other nigga slice my cake did you? I mean, you'd be well within your rights to do so. I'm just wonderin'," I asked. My jealous mind didn't want to know, but my inner alpha male needed to know if anyone had invaded my territory.

"It's still all yours, Gary. You just have to earn the key," he smiled.

"Yeah, but you ain't let no other nigga hit, did you?" I said wanting him to answer the question with a truthful yes or no answer.

"Gary. No! I haven't had sex with anyone but you, okay?" he said holding up his right hand and rolling his eyes.

"My baby. Alright, I can sleep easy now. Minus this hard dick," I said kissing him on the forehead. "But you don't care nothing about this huge problem I have, do you?"

"Well you got 15 good gay minutes to jack off," he laughed sitting back down in the chair.

"I'ma fuck you up," I said laughing and wheeling his lil' ass up to the desk. "Well, hurry up then and come let me rub on your booty at least, damn." Looks like I was going to have to rub one out. Well at least for tonight, anyway. Hell, I was just happy to be able to scoop him up in my arms again. But, I was gonna have to find out how to shorten this probation time he was trying to put me on.

First Impressions Are a Mother...

"What's poppin'?" Michael said answering the phone.

"I am so over it," I said. I was sitting in rush hour traffic coming from the south side.

"What are you over now Jason?" he chuckled.

"I suck at life right now," I said slamming on the brakes to avoid hitting the car ahead of me.

"What's going on?" Michael laughed.

"My barber neglected to call me and tell me that the owner of the shop failed to pay the electricity bill. So I get all the way down on the south side and the shop is sitting in the dark. One of the dudes was there letting folk know what was going on," I paused and grabbed the phone because the call waiting beeped in. "And guess who this is calling me right now?" I said eyeing the phone and sucking my teeth.

"Who your barber?" Michael laughed.

"Exactly. AGH! Ain't this about a female dog? Probably gon' leave a tired ol' message talking about can I come through tomorrow. So now, not only did I not get a cut, but now I have to fight this traffic, and get to the bank on time to meet up with the dude who bought my car. I still need to go to the grocery store, get Batman to the groomer by five, and clean up the house before my mom gets in. And I still wanted to go get a work out in."

"What time does she get in?"

"She'll be in at 8:35. I'm over it," I said in exasperation.

"Jason, calm down, it's only 3:12. You'll get what you need done."

"I just need to vent. I'm really mad because I couldn't get an edge up. And I wasted all this time and gas coming down here. You know what? I'm gonna look for a new barbershop to go too. I'm gonna find a white barber who knows how to hook a taper up."

"That only exists in the movies sad to say," Michael said.

"Well at least one who avoids getting a letter from ComEd saying PAST DUE! Idiot."

"You are a mess. I would help, but I'm on duty tonight. Why don't you have your boyfriend Javier take the dog to get groomed. That way it's one less thing you have to worry about."

"That's not my boyfriend," I snapped.

"Okay, your new fuck-buddy," Michael laughed.

"Shut up!" I laughed. "I had to end our... um... we are no longer together like that anymore," I said switching lanes.

"What happened with ya'll?" Michael asked.

"I got back with Gary," I said as he started coughing. I smiled to myself at his reaction.

"You back with Gary?" he said coughing and clearing his throat. "Boy, you got me choking on my soda."

"Yes, I'm back with Gary," I said.

"You sneaky bitch. And how long has this been going on? That's why your fast ass been MIA, ain't it?"

"It's been a couple of weeks now. I'm going to give him another chance," I said shaking my head and smiling.

"So I guess he gon' meet your mama too, huh?" he asked.

"Of course. So I need you to be on your best behavior at dinner," I warned.

"Since Mama Williams will be in town, I'll see what I can do to limit the shade towards him," he said sucking his teeth.

"Thank you, that's all I ask," I laughed.

"Enjoy the low-life while you can," he said quoting a line from Waiting to Exhale.

"I just want everything to be perfect, Michael. You know?"

"Jason, it will be. Just calm down. This is your mother. It's not a first date, boy."

"I know, but this is a big deal. I don't want her to have a bad taste in her mouth about anything. You know?"

"Jason, if I know you. And I do know you, your house is not a pigsty, and you probably don't even need a damn haircut. You're stressing over nothing. And you went grocery shopping with me this weekend."

"I know I did, but I was going to cook dinner tonight. I wanted to broil some salmon," I said sucking my teeth. I had this picture perfect idea of what the dinner would look like with little place settings and casual adult conversation with mother and son. It looked like the idea I had in my head would be ruined. The perfectionist in me was fighting against this logic.

"You really are bourgeois. And you worse than me with your over planning," Michael said.

"Shut the hell up!" I said laughing. I glanced over at the clock.

"Well, calm down. Just go to the bank. Handle the dog, and take your mom out to dinner tonight. Hell, she may not even be hungry," he laughed.

"Okay, okay," I said taking a deep breath. I regained my composure and put things back into perspective. There was a bigger issue at hand that needed to be addressed more so than the aesthetics of things.

"Are you feeling better now?"

"Kind of," I said trying to believe my own statement.

"Good. I will call you later to check on you. I need to go and muster for duty," Michael said. "Relax and breathe, Jason."

"Okay. I'll talk to you later," I felt a lot better after speaking with my best friend.

I rushed through the remainder of my errands before my mama's arrival. I was nervous for some reason and went through a massive checklist of things

I felt a need to complete. I did everything accept place mints on the pillows in the guest bedroom.

By the time I got dressed, it was 8:08. I took a breather on the couch and prepared myself mentally for Mama's arrival. I did a once over of my place, straightened out a picture frame in the living room, grabbed my keys and headed to the garage. I unlocked the car and heard the pitter patter of Batman following behind me. I sucked my teeth, picked his little butt up and placed him in his kennel. I was now ready to leave. I dialed up Keyshia Cole's new album on my iPod, plugged it into the console, and backed out of the garage. I think I was as ready as I'd ever be. Wow, my mama was coming to see me. I was smiling so hard that it almost turned into a giggle as the excitement rushed through me. I got down the street and realized that I needed to get some gas. The light came on and I laughed to myself, thinking, great one more thing to take care of.

I got the gas and made it to Midway airport with little to no time to spare. I parked the car and rushed my way to the baggage claim area. I checked the teleprompters to make sure her flight was on time, and it was. I had made a sign with Mrs. Williams written on it. I was scanning the crowd walking through the area, and spotted her. I began waving the sign in the air. A wave of emotion hit me as she walked up to me and hugged me. It felt like the time she hugged me goodbye when I was leaving for boot camp. I could feel the love in her arms. That was what I needed to reassure me of her love. It was that moment I knew, that this was real. It was calming. My nervousness dissolved like the vapor exiting the steam holes of an iron. For the first time that day, I believed it was going to be a great week.

"Hey boy!" she said. She was studying me from head to toe as if I were being inspected. It was as if she were looking at me through new lenses.

"Mama, it's good to see you. You look good lady! This is nice," I said complimenting her. She had cut her hair and gave it a little color for added pizzazz.

"You do too. I'm glad you got some hair on your head," she said rubbing my hair.

"I'm growing it out again," I smiled feeling like a little boy.

"Why you waving this sign in the air? Embarrassing me?" she laughed.

"For comic relief," I said.

"Well it worked, silly," she said adjusting the collar on my shirt.

"Okay, let's get your bags and start this adventure," I said rubbing my hands together as we made our way to the carousel.

"Are you hungry?" I asked.

"I could eat something," she said. She was still staring at me like I was new to her.

"Well, I was going to cook, but I ran out of time. So we can go to a sit down restaurant and eat. Do you have a taste for anything in particular?" I said looking over at her.

"Some pasta or something," she said.

"Okay, we can go to Maggiano's. It's an Italian joint. Have you ever been?"

"I've seen the one in Texas, but I haven't been yet. I didn't know that was an Italian restaurant," Mama said. She reached into her purse and grabbed a cloth to clean her eyeglasses.

"Yeah, It's pretty good food too. You'll like it," I said as I pulled my keys out and popped the trunk.

"Well, I hope so. You know I'm picky," she said as we walked up to the car. She placed her glasses back on and adjusted the scarf around her neck.

"Yes. That's where I get it from," I laughed

"When did you get this? I thought you had a two-seater?"

"A few weeks ago. I just sold the other car. I'm going to roll that money into the house. You like it?" I smiled.

"Yeah, this is sharp. It fits you," she said. I placed the bags in the trunk, opened her door, and helped her get in. I walked over to the driver's side and did the same.

"What is Jasmine going to do for turkey day?" I asked.

"She was going to stay with your Daddy. His ass is supposed to fix her car for her, but he up in Detroit. I'm letting her use my car while I'm out here."

"What? You let her drive your car?" I said laughing.

"She has strict guidelines to adhere too," Mama smiled and glanced over at me.

"I know that's right," I said.

"She's going to have dinner over her boyfriend's mother's house. When is the last time you talked with her?"

"I called her yesterday. I told her I was going to send her some stuff for the baby next week."

"What stuff?"

"I bought some clothes and a couple pairs of shoes this weekend. I hope she can fit them. I got the shoes one size bigger and a size 3T for the clothes."

"That should last for a minute. With her little greedy butt. She thinks every time she goes into the kitchen she supposed to get something."

"Just like Jasmine," I laughed.

"I can pack that stuff in my suitcase and take it back with me."

"Oh yeah, duh," I said laughing at myself. "What's wrong with her car?" I asked.

"She needs some new brakes. They're starting to grind. And I think he said something about she warped the rotors. I don't know," she said waving her hand in the air.

"So you're thinking about Dallas?" I asked. We had talked briefly about her moving there when I went to visit. She was comfortable with Texas and had taken a liking to the Dallas Forth Worth area. She and my dad had taken weekend trips there a few times before things got rocky.

"That's the plan for now. It will be home once I close on that house I was telling you about. I refused the counter offer and no one else is willing to pay what they're asking. So far I have the upper hand," she said nodding her head.

"When are you going to know if you got it or not?" I asked.

"Hopefully, next week. That would be a nice Christmas present to myself."

"That really would be," I said. "What about the house in Killeen?"

"We were renting that house. We were supposed to be buying a house, so it'll be your daddy's problem. I don't care."

"Well Ma, I'm really glad you came. You have no idea," I said changing the subject. My heart rate increased as the joy I felt surfaced again.

"Well you only get one mother and I heard what you said that day that you sat me down to talk, and if this is hard for me, I want you to imagine what your daddy is going through?" she said. I glanced over at her and smiled nodding my head.

"I just want ya'll in my life. I don't want to feel like I have to keep my distance from ya'll. I know my life is a hard pill to swallow, but if you could imagine what I had to go through in dealing with it, you all would have a different outlook on things. I'm tired of hiding. You know?" I said sincerely.

"Jason, I get it," she said.

"Okay, I'm sorry, I'm just venting," I smiled.

"None of your friends are drag queens or nothing like that, are they?" she said inquisitively. It was an innocent question, and I had prepared myself for much worse. I wanted her to be comfortable enough to ask whatever she could possibly think of.

"Not at all, Mama. Not in my circle of friends," I laughed. An image of Shawn dressing up in drag for Halloween popped into my head. I chuckled to myself and decided to keep that tidbit of information concealed.

"Well, you don't do any of that mess, do you? Wearing...dresses?"

"Oh God no! I'm not that gay, Ma," I laughed. "I'm scared of drag queens as a matter of fact?" I said, now feeling weird talking to her about this. "How you see me now and when I come home is how I am all the time."

"Well, there was that time I caught you in my canary yellow pumps," she snickered. She was referring to the time I decided to see what the big deal was about women's shoes. I tried on a pair of her best heels and walked up and down the hallway laughing at myself thinking about how silly I looked. My mom just so happened to come home early from work that day and caught me in them. She made me wear them until just before my dad was due home from work. She sent me on errands throughout the house and forced me to vacuum the living room four consecutive times, among other things. She was more or less entertaining herself by laughing at me trying to maintain my balance while clumsily maneuvering the massive Kirby upright we owned. Perhaps this is why I didn't like drag queens, I thought.

"You would remember that of all things, Ma," I said laughing. I never again had the desire to even think about wearing any type of garment or footwear designed for a female since that traumatic childhood experience. It was hilarious to me now.

"Why are you scared of drag queens?" she laughed. I had her full undivided attention.

"It's just a little weird to me. Even though they share the same community as I, it's just something strange and out there about a dude in a dress. It's too many people sharing one body. I can't explain it," I laughed. I never really thought about the reasons behind it. The only drag queen I was ever comfortable around was the one I had built a rapport with in Wilmington, North Carolina, at Club Ibiza. And I couldn't even remember her name.

We got to the restaurant and were seated rather quickly. The place wasn't very busy. The waitress came and took our drink orders and gave us time to sift through the menu. We placed the order, sipped our drinks, and continued the conversation. It was strangely refreshing opening up to my mom.

"So what can I expect from your friends? Who are they and what are they like?" she said folding her arms on the table.

"Okay, let's see," I said taking a moment to brainstorm the best image of the crew. "Well, there is Michael, Shawn, and Preston. We've all been friends since 2000. I met them all when I was stationed at Camp Lejuene. Michael is originally from Atlanta, Georgia. He's still in the Navy and is the oldest of the bunch. He's a Mama's boy with a love for church among other things," I laughed. I couldn't tell her about his favorite past time. "Shawn is a country boy from Virginia. He used to be in the Marine Corps. He is in school studying Sociology and works at the electric company out here. He's a ball of energy and is the party guy of the group. Then there is Preston, who recently finished studying at the Art institute. He's doing an internship with a fashion design firm in the city. He is sort of the stereotypical gay dude of the group, but he isn't overly flamboyant. Shawn is going to be out of town, so you are only going to get to meet Michael and Preston at dinner Thursday.

"Okay. Sounds interesting," Mama said nodding her head. I could hear the wheels turning in her head. I only wanted to give her a snap shot of the boys and let her form her own opinions of them after she met them.

"Why you say it like that?" I laughed taking a sip of my water.

"No. I'm painting a mental picture of them in my head, boy," she laughed and took a sip of her water. "I was just wondering if you've dated any of these guys?"

"No. These guys are my brothers to me. We are strictly friends and those are the pretenses we met under," I stated plainly. I know that a lot of same gender loving men that are friends have slept with one another before becoming just friends.

"I just know how your Uncle Jessie was. That's the only example I have."

"Not to mention what the media brain washes the public into thinking we all are?" I said adding my two cents. "We're not all AIDS patients, Ma."

"So you're not having sex all the time with any and everybody, are you?" She asked.

"Oh my God, Ma. No, I'm not promiscuous if that's what you're asking," I said. "I admit, just like straight people, there are gays that are heavy into sex, but I'm not one of those people. Stop looking at what you see on T.V.," I laughed.

"Yeah. T.V. perpetuates a lot of stereotypes about all people."

"It can be unfair sometimes. We aren't all flamboyant either," I chuckled. There was a slight break in the conversation as we looked over the menu.

I used to wonder if it would have been easier for my parents to accept the fact that I preferred men if I were effeminate. It's easy to embrace a stereotype as opposed to the truth, because there is no effort needed in understanding it. It's simply an ideal passed down until it's challenged with the truth. It's perpetuated until it's questioned with a curious desire to be enlightened.

I tried my hardest to be a non-stereotypical black man while embracing black culture in its entirety and a non-stereotypical same gender loving black male at the same time. I feel that since men like me exist; we have a responsibility to curtail certain stereotypes from the media and society. I had to do it while in the Navy, more or less becoming a chameleon. In that type of environment, it can be a matter of survival.

I represent a facet of the community that cannot be denied. The more in their face I am, the more I can show that the black gay male is available for more than comic relief. A masculine same gender lover is deemed a threat to the fabric of masculinity. My family and straight counterparts do not understand me, so by blotting out a representation of my image from the media or one's mind, I don't exist. I am not the safe individual like my more effeminate peers. I offer confusion to society and pose the question of conversion since I look the part of my heterosexual peers.

For years, I wondered if my folks felt like this. Since I didn't look or act gay according to what they know gay to be, why couldn't I just make the switch? I don't know if this was something I could get them to understand. I was surely going to make an effort to drive this point home. It took a while to climb my own truth tree and I wasn't going to climb back down from it.

"Sooo...are you dating someone?" she said clearing her throat. It was as if she was bracing herself for the answer.

"Could you handle it if I were? I know meeting my friends could be a big step for you. I wanted to ease you into my life," I said.

"Would I rather it be a girl, yes, but I'm here to deal with it...that you like men," she said giving me direct eye contact.

"Cool. I mean, Mama, I just don't want something to happen to me one day. God Forbid," I paused and looked up to the sky. "And you get a call from one of my friends telling you about me being in an accident and you don't know who they are. Not to mention you giving a generic eulogy at my funeral." I said.

"I understand, Jason. That's why I'm here. You have to understand that for me, I had to mourn the death of a child so to speak. So I'm seeing you in a new light. My thoughts, and dreams, and the life I envisioned for my son didn't include you being gay. So

I'm having to restructure my image of you. This is new to me."

"I know, Ma," I smiled. "Having the freedom to discuss this with you is new to me."

"Now who is this boy you're seeing?" she smiled. "I can't believe I'm asking my son that question," she said shaking her head and chuckling. She closed her eyes and squeezed the bridge of her nose with her index finger and thumb. She then grabbed her glass and took a gulp of water.

"I know, right?" I said laughing at her embarrassment. This was a lot for me to take on because I'm so used to fighting about this whole gay thing, so now to not endure any resistance was a bit odd. "Okay, his name is Gary Larrieux," I said grabbing my phone. "I have a picture of him." I pulled my pictures up and handed her the phone.

"Mmm hmph," she said adjusting her eyeglasses.

"His family is originally from the Bahamas. He was born there, but he was raised here in Chicago." I said wondering what was going through her head. In spite of what he and I went through, I was proud to actually have someone worth her being able to meet. There was no need to go into all of our ins and out this past year, because it seemed we were picking up where we'd left off. I just hoped she would like him.

"Hmph. I'm just glad he ain't some white guy?" she said smiling. She started going through the other pics I had in my iPhone. "You ever heard the expression, if they can't use your comb, don't bring them home?"

"Yeah, I think I've heard that before," I said laughing and shaking my head.

"Well, at least he's attractive. You need to teach your sister how to find someone worth looking twice at," she said handing me my phone.

"I know, right?" I laughed.

"Thank God Aaliyah turned out pretty. What's his name again?"

"Gary Larreiux. You are going to meet him tomorrow. We're taking you sightseeing around the city, and I know you want to get some shopping done."

"Well, tell me about him."

"Well, he is a Fire Fighter for the city. He's working on getting this big promotion at his job. He's 6'1, he's a masculine guy, and he's family oriented and very close to his parents. He's an outdoorsy type of guy. He's pretty well rounded and good to me. And he knows Jesus. I think that you will like him."

"Let's hope so," Mama said.

Mama and I continued talking over dinner followed by dessert. We laughed, joked, and grilled each other about everything. It was nice having a genuine adult, no holds barred conversation with my mom. I couldn't have asked for a better blessing. She listened to me wholeheartedly and asked what I can imagine were some pretty difficult questions for her.

Me being blunt told the truth and poured my heart out to her. It was therapeutic for the two of us, especially when she opened up about how hurt she was with what went down with her and Daddy. I explained to her that I could somewhat empathize with her while explaining what happened between Gary and me. We shared a hearty laugh when she said, "I guess men can be dogs gay or straight."

I told my Momma how much her being here meant to me. I no longer held resentment towards her somewhat disowning me. She cried and told me she felt where I was coming from. She was also crying because I was gay and there was nothing she could do about it. Her fears are of how God will perceive me, how the majority of the world is against me, and how she couldn't protect and shield me from its hate any longer. She told me that we are living in a time where we need to realize we need to love one another unconditionally. Mama said she would leave it at that because that's the love Jesus has for us.

I let her know I learned how to fight and pray from her. I also let her know that I learned strength from her. Mama told me that she could see that in spite of it all. She could see that she didn't mess me up completely, expressing how she did something right. She explained how she doesn't understand my attraction to the same sex, but she needs to get over it if she wants me completely in her life. I told her I didn't understand the attraction I have for dudes either. It's just how I was programmed. We left it at that and went to bed. This was the most emotion I have ever witnessed from my mother and I think this was the most emotion I have ever shown her. I can truly say I now have an understanding and appreciation for a mother's love. This is all I've ever wanted from her.

In Geometry, one learns that the quickest way to a destination is a straight line. The chicane between the two of us created to avoid certain topics and feelings is now a straight-a-way. My mama is back on my team. Thank you God.

Temptation Is Your Friend...

The visit from my mom was initially a shock to me. I didn't think that I would ever see the day that she would ever come and spend time with me under my own roof, let alone say some of the most loving things to me as she did. It was as if I were being liberated from matrilineal purgatory. For so long I felt like she didn't like me or maybe only tolerated me for the sake of me owning the title of son. I no longer felt like the wayward child in her eyes.

It's amazing how so many years lost can be dissolved by just a few moments of taking the time out to capture the now. Moving forward I know that she loves me, and though we still have some work to do within the healing process of our relationship, I am no longer mad at her. I love her and can say that without saying it out of necessity.

Her interaction with my friends was wonderful. She wasn't indifferent towards them, and I was able to see a different side of her as she asked them questions about their lives and about our friendship. Michael embarrassed me by telling a few of my secrets, one being the time I accidentally cursed in his home church when the choir got up to sing my favorite gospel song. He had us rolling as he recalled that day and mimicked me loudly proclaiming, "Oh shit, that's my SONG!" I was mortified that day and wanted to stand up, raise my index finger, and excuse myself from the remainder of service.

It was things like this that gave my mother insight into how unique I was. We told stories of how we all met and how Michael didn't like me initially because he thought I was arrogant and pretentious. I told her I got it honest and she agreed and came to my rescue. She let Michael know that she raised her children to want more out of life than just the status quo. She wanted us to be educated and proud of whom we were and own it because no one could take that away, not even her.

Spending time with her and my friends is something I will treasure always. I hoped that she could say the same thing. I didn't want her to leave because there was so much more that I wanted to share and experience with her during her visit, but as the old cliché goes, all great things in life must come to an end.

I drove back to my place from the airport in silence letting my mind wander. I thought about Mama's interaction with Gary and how the two of them seemed to hit it off. He told her that I looked so much like her; all I needed was long hair. He also pulled her to the side and discussed how much he loved me to her. He said to her, that he was going to give me the world, and take really good care of her son. He said that she in turn told him that I was her only son and that she still had her issues with this, but she was getting past all of that. He had me laughing when he said she grabbed his collar and pulled him down to her level and threatened to pull his "dick string" out if she finds out that he hurt me again. What a "dick string" is is unbeknownst to me, but for as long as I can remember, she's been using that threat against me and my dad.

It's funny how you can pray about something for years, trusting and believing that it will come to past and when it unexpectedly does, you question it. I wish that I could see what was going on in her head from all that she witnessed on this visit. What was she anticipating? What are her views now of me and my quote unquote lifestyle? Were her judgments truly gone? And is that Darius walking up to my front door? Yes, it was. I pulled into the driveway and pressed the button on the remote for the garage door to open. Darius smiled as I drove past.

"Wow, what the hell are you doing here?" I said stepping out and shutting the car door. Darius walked into the garage.

"I'm here to see the brotha who lives here? He owes me a hug. You know him?" Darius said. He looked good as hell with his ol' chocolate self.

"Yeah, you're looking at him," I smiled.

"Well come here sir and pay what you owe," Darius said giving me a bear hug.

"What's up? When did you get back?" I said taking in the scent of his cologne.

"I got in yesterday afternoon. I'm staying with my pops."

"Cool, well let's get inside. It's cold out here. I said closing the garage door.

"I see somebody's balling out of control. This shits tight! When did you get that?"

"A few weeks ago. It's my Christmas and birthday present to myself. It's cool," I said as we walked into the house.

"Yeah it is," he said.

"Here, give me your coat," I hung my coat and his in the closet. I then walked over and let Batman out of the bathroom. He ran past me and started barking at Darius. "Batty boy chill out. Stop it now. Come here," I said tapping my leg with my hand.

"He mad at me, huh? Like who is this strange nigga in my house," Darius joked.

"He'll be alright in a minute. I had a few people over for the holidays, so he's been a little territorial," I said as Batman followed me over to the fridge. I grabbed two bottles of Vitamin Water. "You want one?"

"Nope. I hate them things. You got regular water?" he said sitting at the table.

"Yeah, here you go," I said tossing him a bottle.

"Cool, so what's up baby boy?" he was smiling ear to ear as he twisted the cap off of the water.

"I could ask you that same question," I said leaning up against the counter." Batman jumped up on my leg. I went and got him a treat and poured some water in his dish. I walked back over to the counter and propped myself up.

"I'm good. I'm just glad to be home."

"Is this R&R or are you back for good?"

"I'm back for good. I'm going back to D.C. next Wednesday."

"You ready?" I said.

"Yeah, I'm ready. I get to put my research together and present it to the powers that be. It's been a pretty good exercise."

"That's what's up?" I said taking a sip of my drink.

"So how many niggas you been wildin' out with now that you are a bachelor and shit?" Darius asked. He was looking around the kitchen.

"You would ask that question. I ain't been wildin' out, boy," I said rolling my eyes. Batman walked over to me and laid down by my foot.

"Yeah right! So you just been a little saint all this time you been single?" he laughed giving me the side eye.

"I ain't sayin' all that. I just ain't been buck wild like you're thinking. What's up with you and ol' girl? Better question," I said raising an eyebrow.

"She a'ight. We ain't like that. She was just some ass while I was over there," Darius smiled. I sucked my teeth.

"You're so full of crap. Not to mention a whore bag. You confused boys are something else. You're getting to old to be straddling the fence you know." I said shaking my head.

"What? I can't have the best of both worlds?" he smiled. Darius shrugged his shoulders and gave me that little innocent boyish smile of his that I missed.

"Anyway! According to your email, ho, you were all in this girls behind. It seemed like she had your nose all open. What happened?"

"Jason, I don't know. I was just doing whatever. We just got close, and you know, it is what it is," he shrugged his shoulders and recapped the water bottle. "I think maybe I was trying to keep up appearances and seeing if I still had it. She got a fiancé anyway. So she's out there foul. I guess I took advantage of the situation. She threw the pussy at me and I beat."

"Wow! Come on, let's go into the living room," I said shaking my head. "I'm glad your back," I slapped him on the back.

"I'm glad you still got back. Damn, that ass is right," he said looking over my shoulder.

"Well, that's off limits, Fido."

"You shittin' me!" he said sitting down. Batman followed and lay in his doggy bed.

"How is your dad doing?"

"Yeah, the old man is good, Jay. How are your peoples?"

"Man, everybody is fine. I had my mom up for Turkey day. She really enjoyed herself. We were able to hash some things out, and she met me halfway. She met the crew and everything, it was really a blessed holiday for me man. I even talked to my dad for a hot minute."

"Cool, I'm glad to hear that. Sounds like your life is on the up and up then?" he finished the rest of   the water in one gulp before smashing the bottle into his palm and recapping it.

"Yeah, it looks that way. I'm enjoying life. Livin' it up," I said doing a little dance.

"You gon' give me a tour of the place?" Darius said.

"Oh yeah. It ain't much but it's mine," I said modestly.

"I like it so far. How many bedrooms is it?"

"It's a three bedroom," I said, as we made our way upstairs.

"Oh so cool, I can stay with you from time to time, huh?" Darius asked.

"I don't know about all that. I can't just let anybody lay up in my crib," I said joking with him.

"I'm not just anybody, ol' curly cue head face ass."

"Shut the hell up, ol' closet case face ass. So lame, you can't even pick a gender," I said as we both laughed.

"I see you still know how to play the face ass game," Darius laughed.

"You so stupid. So anyway, here is my lil' office area and junk. I still have a few more things I want to do to it. I saw a better bookcase at this store downtown I want to pick up."

"Okay, nice. How you like your Mac?" he asked observing my computer.

"I love it. I still haven't really tapped into all you can do with it. But Macs are the ish! Why, you thinking about getting one?"

"I have an iBook. I don't know yet. I still do a lot of stuff on the work computer you know."

"Well, they have a conversion software program so you can go from PC to Mac and vice versa. You should look into it."

"Yeah, I will, cause I like my laptop," Darius said.

"Okay, so this is the guest bedroom. I just put the finishing touches on it not too long ago."

"I likes, I likes," he said nodding his head.

"And here is my bedroom," I said as we walked further down the hallway.

"Yes! This is where it goes down, huh?" he said rubbing his hands together.

"Not so much, silly." "Shiiiiid!" he laughed.

"This is a pure and innocent place. Holy and sanctified in the name of Jesus," I said pretending to do a church shout. He walked over to my nightstand.

"Yeah, with this big economy sized bottle of lube just chillin'. This must be your holy oil," he said holding up my lube.

"Boy, put that down. Give me that," I said walking over to him and snatching it out of his hand. I laughed and sat it back down. "It is a pretty nice size bottle though."

"I'm just saying, not so innocent to me," he chuckled putting his fist up to his mouth.

"Whatever," I said as he grabbed my arm. "Come here. Jay, I missed you," he said bear hugging me.

"I can't tell," I said trying to resist temptation.

"Well, I did," he said holding me in his arms. He kissed the side of my face.

"That's cool. I missed you too, gay boy." "According to my email, I'm straight," he smiled.

"Yeah, straight like 6:15 on an analog clock," I laughed.

"Oh you a funny guy now, huh?"

"Yup. Alright, let's get back downstairs," I said trying to escape his grip. I was starting to feel guilty about letting him touch me the way he was. A part of me was receptive to it, but the logical side of me was telling me to stop before temptation gets the better of you.

"Am I making you nervous or something?" he smiled not letting go.

"We're passed that. I can't be up here with you like this," I said.

"So what I can't hold you no more," he said moving in for a kiss.

"You can't be kissing on me, Dee," I said repositioning my head.

"I don't see why not," he said. Just then I could hear my phone ringing downstairs.

"Yo', I need to take that. That's probably, my man," I said as I broke free from his embrace. I darted down the stairs and grabbed my phone from the kitchen counter. "Hello"

"What up, babes? You at home?" Gary asked. I heard Darius walk downstairs towards the living room.

"Yeah, I'm at home."

"Mama on the plane safe?" he asked as I tried to catch my breath.

"Yeah, she's on the way back. I told her to call me later when she lands," I said trying to switch the phone to my other ear. But it slipped out of my hands. I reached down to pick it up.

"Hello! Babes, what happened? You alright?" Gary laughed.

"Yeah, I just dropped the phone," I said.

"See you dropping stuff, you sure you alright? You know how you get when you're nervous. What's going on over there?" Darius had walked into the kitchen at that point and grabbed another bottle of water out of the refrigerator.

"I'm good, boo, seriously." I laughed nervously hoping he didn't hear Darius enter the kitchen.

"I'm looking forward to some alone time with you tonight."

"I can hear it in your voice," I smiled. I wanted to rush him off the phone without rushing him off the phone. I didn't feel right talking in front of Darius.

"Yeah, just me and my babes," Gary said.

"You ain't getting none tonight though," I teased. Darius smiled at me shook his head and headed into the living room.

"Hell yes I am. But yo' I gotta get back to work. I'm taking you out tonight so we can celebrate our exclusivity. So you just look real sexy and let your man handle the rest. Cool?"

"I'm looking forward to it."

"Alright so say around six."

"Six o'clock. I'll be ready," I smiled.

"Alright babes, I gotta finish up here. See you tonight, alright."

"Alright, don't work too hard and stress out."

"I'm on cloud nine right now. I'm not trippin' on stress."

"Cool," I said.

"Jason," Gary said. "Yes?"

"You can trust me, alright?'

"I'd better be able too," I said. "See you soon."

"Bye bye," I said as Gary hung up. I walked into the living room. Darius was flipping through the channels. He smiled as I walked in.

"So who is this mystery nigga? Do I know him?" he asked giving me the side eye.

"Kind of sort of," I said rolling my eyes and taking a seat.

"Who is it?"

"The dude you fought in the club last time you were home."

"GREGORY?!" he said in disbelief.

"It's GARY! Yeah. You know his name," I smiled.

"Aww nigga, you trying to be on an episode of Cheaters, and shit?! You really took that ol' bogus fool back?" he laughed.

"Shut the hell up, boy! Yes, I took him back," I said laughing at his comment.

"I'm just joking. I'm not trying to offend your man," he laughed. He rolled his neck like a ghetto girl.

"Thank you. Respect my man," I said throwing a pillow at him.

"Damn, okay. Ya'll two together again," he said rubbing his chin. "Dude better not fuck you over this time or I'm really going kill him. I knew this was going to happen," he said sucking his teeth and shaking his head.

"Well, I'm glad I got your approval," I stated. It felt good to know that he was still protective of me.

"Well, I wish you would have waited on me, but hey," he smiled.

"Darius, ain't enough time in the freakin' world for that. We just need to be real and call what you and I have what it is - friendship. We are destined to be just friends," I said clasping my hands together.

"We are attracted to each other like water and shores," he said cheesing really hard.

"I mean... you still got a cute thing happenin'. But I have to keep you at bay," I said smiling.

"Nigga, I would nail that ass to the floor right now if you weren't with ol' dude," he said staring at me. I had to admit the visual thought of his comment was hot as hell.

"You can't have everything you want," I said trying to play it off as if his statement didn't faze me.

"Aww, Jason, you of all people know not to challenge me," he said placing his arm on the back of the couch.

"Alright, I'm changing the subject," I said avoiding eye contact with him. If I didn't, he would serve up the most delicious guilty pleasure known to gay men: sexual temptation.

"That's right you know what's up!" Darius said nodding his head. He twisted the cap off of the water bottle placing it to his lips. He turned the bottle up and finished the remaining contents.

"Do I now?" I chuckled.

"Sure do," he said. He crushed the bottle and recapped it.

"Your pompous ass," I said, shaking my head.

"Don't hate. That's not a good look."

"Neither is breast feeding," I said reaching for my drink.

"You should try out a pair. You might like

them."

"My mama tried breast feeding me when I was a baby. It didn't work then and it ain't gonna work now," I said.

"Faggot," Darius smiled.

"Thank you. I appreciate the compliment," I said taking a gulp of my drink. "You know what that means right?"

"What, faggot?" he asked.

"Yup! It means, Fellow Accepting God's Gifts on Time. F.A.G.G.O.T." I stated confidently reciting my own interpretation of the word. Darius shook his head and laughed at my creativity.

I always felt some kind of way about Darius, even when I was with Gary. I never could put my finger on it. I passed it off as a crush; another dude I thought was cute, but it truly was so much more than that. Today when he finally made me take a much closer look at he and I, it dawned on me he had been single the entire time I've known him. I met him nearly four years ago, and it was just something about him I couldn't shake. I was with Gary but isolated a lot of the time. We were both on the self-improvement track while trying to maintain a healthy relationship.

I discovered that ninety-nine percent of the time you look, you run into someone who is just as lonely as you are. You may stare this person in the face with brevity from time to time and get a warm fuzzy without consciously recognizing it. Then, it just clicks, and out of the blue you find that you are meant for each other. The chemistry finally becomes right. Kindred spirits finally claim one another. It's a different level of timing. Not something man could conjure up. Gary and I probably didn't realize what we had the first time around, but that all changed that night, as he shared a poem he'd written for me. One of the first poems he'd ever done. It wasn't cheesy and definitely not something I thought he'd come up with in a million years. The last part was really amazing and further sealed the deal for me. It read:

... I studied your face the first time we made love,
Studied as I would any test, But this one of time.
For I see plenty of years with you. I'm glad I kept believing,
I almost let go as if grieving,
Now simply you I'm receiving,
While enjoying Alicia play them keys,
Your rhythmic beauty comes to life gingerly rocking me to sleep.
Your heartbeat, My heartbeat,
Replaces the thump, Tap,
Splat,
of our facial rainfall.
Were we ever apart to begin with...?

Pill Popping Pillow Fights...

"I'm going to wear this to the funeral. I think. What do you think of this tie?" Michael asked. He held it up against a shirt he'd picked out.

"I like it. You're not feeling it?" I asked. I was ironing a pair of dress pants for him.

"I don't know. I'm torn between this one and this one. I like this one because it has more pink in it. That was her favorite color," he was admiring the ties he laid out across his bed.

"I like that one. On your right, plus you have the handkerchief to go with it. And you can wear those shoes with it," I said pointing in his closet.

"Yeah, you have a point," Michael said taking a gulp of his Apple Martini."

"Michael, slow down please with the liquor."
"Jason. I got this okay!" he said with a stern look. I shook my head.

"Michael, you have been really on a roll with this whole alcohol thing lately. It's not cool for you to be pounding drinks down like you've been doing," I said continuing to push the issue.

"Boy, I'll be fine! Can you please do me a favor and get my blue suitcase out of the storage closet for me? I'm good. Stop bitching at me about this alcohol!" Michael scoffed.

"Alright. I'm just being a concerned friend. I'm sorry," I said sitting the iron down.

"Be a friend and get the suitcase, please," Michael said without looking at me.

"Be right back," I said. I walked out onto his patio. I opened the storage unit and grabbed the bag he requested. I brought it back, sat it on the bed, and unzipped it. Michael was on the phone with his father.

"Dad, I'm on Continental Airlines... No, sir, Continental! I'm on the first flight of the morning... 6:48... Jason... Yeah, he's here with me now... Jason, my dad says hello... "

"Tell him I said, 'Hello."

"He says 'hello'... I'm trying to be strong Dad. I don't think it's really hit home yet. I just talked to her the night before last, and she was... Oh Jesus... I can't believe it... I just talked to her... I don't understand... I know she is... Yes, sir... Yes, sir... You alright? Well, let me finish up here, and I will call you later tonight? Yes, sir... Bye."

"Is he doing alright?" I asked.

"He seems to be holding up pretty well. Jason... I can't do this. I can't do this. I cannot fucking do this!" Michael said punching the wall. He sat down on the floor. I walked over and tried to console him.

"Shhhh. Michael, breathe man. Let it out. It's okay," I said as Michael hugged me, and started sobbing.

"No, no, no, no, no, no NO! LORD! Why it has to be her, Jason? Why he take my mama, Jason? I need her man! I need her right now." He was pointing at his chest, and shouting up at the ceiling. "All I'm going through! I NEED HER! I need her man, I need my momma! I need her! It wasn't time for her yet! It wasn't fucking time..." he said sobbing.

"I know, dude. I know. Death isn't on anyone's schedule. But we all have to go home when God calls. She's still with you, okay? She's with God, and he'll make sure that she continues to look after you."

"I know. It's not fair, Jason. I need her here on Earth. I don't want to send her to..." he stopped talking and just started silently praying, asking God why. I could not begin to imagine the pain or loss he was suffering right now. This was yet another place I could not reach. How could I gain my Mother and he loses his? All I could do was be there for my friend. I went and got a warm washcloth for him and some tissues once he calmed down. He dabbed his face with the tissue and wiped his face with the towel. "Thank you."

"You're welcome," I said.

"Is there such a thing as silence?" he said with a somber look on his face.

"I don't think so because you still hear your heartbeat when you plug up your ears. So I'm going to go out on a limb and say physically no. I don't think there is such thing as silence. Hell, when fire burns it even makes a sound. Why do you ask?" I said not fully understanding his question.

"I hope she can hear me man. That's all. They say the body is a shell, but the spirit lives on. So is the spirit doing the hearing?" Michael asked.

"I don't know. I'll have to think about that one. That's a deep question," I said as he took the last gulp of his cocktail.

"Michael, I'm not going to be up all night making sure you don't die from alcohol poisoning."

"You know what, Jason. Fuck you! You always want to make everything about you. YOU, YOU, YOU! The world does not revolve around your high and mighty ass. If I want to fucking get white-boy wasted, then that's what the fuck I'm going to do!" Michael yelled. His southern accent was always more pronounced when he had liquor in his system.

"Excuse me? I never said that the world revolves around me. What I am saying is, I'm not going to let you drink yourself into a coma and..."

"And what? I am so tired of you reading everybody because you think you know every got-damned thing! I'm sick and tired of your negative comments about the shit we do," he said slapping his hand against his chest. "I'm sick and tired of you acting like your shit don't stink, shawty. You are a fucking mean ass self-centered bitch sometimes. You know that?"

"Michael, what the hell is wrong with you? I am not negative towards any of ya'll. For the record we all offer each other constructive criticism. And I know you aren't talking as controlling and buffoonish as you can act sometimes. All the crap that you are going through is all on you. And you gon' get pissed at me because I call you out on your own bullshit? After you consult me about it? Really, Michael?"

"You got some nerve, bitch! With yo' funky ass attitude! Consult you about it? All you have to worry about is yourself. You got a clean bill of health, you don't have fucking bugs flowing through your precious little veins, you don't have a nigga constantly vandalizing your precious little sports car, you don't have your boss making your life a living hell at work because you won't fuck him! And you don't have to put your mother in the fucking ground either! Selfish muthafucka! If you would open up and stop being so frigid, you wouldn't have to worry about muthafucka's cheating on you. All you do is worry about your damn self," Michael screamed.

"You know you sound real stupid right now! If you would take the time to listen sometimes, you wouldn't be in the situations that you get yourself into. You bring all that crap on yourself. I meant what the hell I said about you and that boy you were messing with. I told you from jump to leave his lil' queeny ass alone. I also told you to stop letting your dick lead you and look what happened. You screwed your supervisor and then played him to the left. How you think he gonna respond? Stop passing dick out like Halloween candy! And if you would cover your dick up with a condom or hell Syran Wrap, for that matter, you wouldn't have to be popping pills and getting penicillin shots. It ain't fair that you raw doggin' these kats knowin' you got something. You getting everything you deserve. Stop being a vindictive WHORE!" I said. I was really failing at trying to control my temper.

"Fuck you!" he said. At this point, his drunkenness had really set in. He took a swing at me. I backed away.

"Michael, I'm not about to fight you boy. Sit your drunk ass down. I'm serious!" I said throwing my hand up to protect myself. He obviously took this as a threat.

"Fuck you, don't bitch out of this ass whoopin'!"

"You know what, I'm out, you figure this crap out on your own. IDIOT!" I said throwing up my arms.

"Don't you walk the fuck away from me! FUCK YOU BITCH!" Michael screamed. He lunged forward, and pushed me. I pushed him back, and he crashed into his computer desk. A few items fell down, and the tray that holds the keyboard bent downward.

"You drunk, ho! Are you crazy?" I yelled.

"According to your bitch ass!" he said getting up. He jumped up and swung at me again. He missed. I pushed him again, and he grabbed my arm. We both crashed to the floor. We were wrestling around for a few seconds before he guts punched me with a few quick jabs. I felt the ironing board fall down on top of us. I saw red and returned two blows to his ribs. He sent one blow to my jaw and I got two swings at his face before we separated. One in the eye, and the other made contact with his mouth. I pushed Michael off of me and leaped to my feet. I was breathing heavy and was beyond pissed. I was livid.

"Bitch, get the fuck out of my house! Punk ass bitch! FUCK YOU!" he said wiping the blood from his lip with his forearm.

"What the hell is wrong with you?" I asked. "We're brothers. We don't do this type of thing to one another," I yelled.

"You think you gon' call me out, so I had to set the record straight," he said. I shook my head nonchalantly avoiding eye contact with him. If I had of looked at him again, it would have taken everything within me not to unleash all the years of suppressed anger from being exerted onto him. I had never been in a fight before.

"Get the fuck out of my house!" Michael yelled.

"Gladly! With your country ass. How the hell you call yourself a top sipping on Apple Martini's anyway?! Late punk!" I said.

"We ain't friends no mo' either bitch! I don't need you! Cancel Christmas bitch!" Michael said following me into the living room. I gathered my belongings in silence, trying to remain as calm as possible. I could not bring myself to look at him.

"When you get sober give me a call. I'm over it! You can walk to the swamps of Georgia for all I care," I said making my way to the door.

"Keep talking all that shit about A-Town bitch! We not gon' talk about that Pleasantville called Detroit, now are we?! I got something for that ass next time I see you sidity muthafucka!" he said flinging a glass at me.

"MICHAEL, THE CARPET IS ON FIRE!" I yelled.

He ran to the back to tend to the flames. I took this as the perfect time to exit this situation. "I hope this raggedy apartment burns the hell down," I said just as the smoke detector went off. I headed downstairs putting on my coat. In all actuality, it was a really nice apartment, but I just had to dish out one more insult in an effort to have the last word.

I got in the car and made my way to the freeway. I checked my face out in the mirror. I was cool. I laughed to myself after I calmed down. This was truly the most childish fight Michael and I have ever had, but we have never laid hands on one another. This was crazy. I didn't know what to expect come next week once he returned home. Who knows if we'd still be friends? I know he was drunk, but we had some deep rooted stuff to talk about supposedly. I know I speak my mind, but I didn't know he felt that I was egregious.

By the time I got to the city, I was completely calm. I made up my mind that I wasn't going to talk to

Michael until he apologized. So let the shade begin! I pulled up to my house, and opened the garage. I pulled my phone out of my pocket and realized I had several missed calls from Michael as well as two text messages from him marked urgent and another missed call from Javi. I sent a text to Javi and told him I'd call him shortly, and then proceeded to call Gary. I figured the texts from Michael were him cursing me out and calling me out of my name.

"What's up babes, what you up too?" Gary asked.

"I just pulled up to the house."

"I thought you were going to spend the night at Michaels."

"We got into a fight."

"What about?"

"Well, apparently I'm this mean judgmental person," I said. I got out of the car and made my way inside.

"What? No, you're not," Gary laughed.

"It's a long story. Where you at?"

"I was on my way to your house to take care of the dog."

"Really?" I said as my call waiting chimed in. It was Michael.

"Um huh, I'm in the car now."

"Cool, you can come on I need one of your hugs. Baby, hang on one second, this is Michael," I said, thinking this had better be him apologizing.

"Okay, babes, hurry back."

"Yes Michael?" I asked clicking over. I was still irritated from earlier.

"I messed up, Jason..." he said. He seemed to be crying. His voice was really shaky and he sounded out of it. My facial expression change immediately and he had my full-undivided attention. I stopped dead in my tracks. Something was not right.

"Michael, you alright, what's wrong?"

"I need...I need help. I...swallowed dem ball...then all. I messed...up!" He was slurring his words.

"Michael, what do you mean you swallowed them all, what's going on? You're scaring me now. What did you do?" I dropped the bag I was holding and noticed my hand was shaking after I realized what the hell he just said.

"Pills, I swallowed...them pills. I messed my life up. I need...help me," Michael said. He started crying.

"Michael. Oh my God, what did you do!? I'm on my way to you now. Please don't hang up, I'm going to get you help, okay! Stay on the phone, okay!" I said frantically running through the house back to the car.

"I messed up...Jason. I'm sorry. I sorry..."

"I know. It's okay. I'm on the way to you, okay?

What did you take, you got to tell me what you took?"

"AIDS pills...pills for that."

"Okay, Michael please hold on. I'm going to click over and get some help, please hold on," I said as I clicked over. Gary was still on the phone.

"Baby, please do me a huge favor. I need you to call 911 and get an ambulance over to Michael's place. He tried to commit suicide. He says he swallowed a bottle of pills."

"Oh my God, babes, okay I'm going to call. What's the address?"

"Um...658 Lakehurst Rd. Apartment # C, in Waukegan. I'm on the way up there now. Did you get the address?"

"Yeah, I got it. Okay, I'm gonna call now and hit you right back!"

"Thank you. I gotta click over, I told him to hang on," I said clicking over. "Michael? MIKE! Are you there? Hello!" I couldn't hear anything but music on the other end. "Michael, if you hear me, I'm on the way. An ambulance is coming too. HELLO! MIKE!"

I tried calling Shawn and got voicemail. I left a message for him to call me ASAP! I clicked back over and screamed Michael's name through the phone. I was speeding through the streets making my way towards the highway. All of a sudden, I heard the dial tone. I connected blue tooth in the car, so that I could concentrate on weaving through the traffic. I called Michael's phone three times, and each time I got nothing but voicemail. I tried Shawn again and got an answer.

"Hello," he answered.

"Shawn, I think that Michael tried to commit suicide. I'm on my way to his place now. An ambulance is on the way," I said coming to a screeching halt at a red light. I leaned forward scanning traffic debating on running the light. My brother was more important than a traffic ticket right now.

"Wait a minute, are you serious?"

"YES! I just got off the phone with him! He's not answering! He told me that he swallowed a bottle of pills," I said. The light turned green and I threw the car in first gear and sped off.

"Oh my God! Okay, I am going to try him, and start heading down that way," Shawn said. Gary chimed in on the call waiting.

"Shawn, I'm gonna call you back," I said swerving around an SUV. "Gary, did you make the call?" I asked.

"The ambulance is on the way to him! Where are you at?"

"I'm about to get on the freeway in a minute."

"You got a key to his place?" Gary asked.

"Yeah, we all have keys to each other's cribs. Baby, I think he passed out or something. He's not answering the phone!" I said.

"Let's be positive, baby. He's alright, and help is on the way."

"What would make him do this? Jesus, PLEASE save my friend! PLEASE!" I stated frantically. I rubbed my hand vigorously across my head, trying to get a grip and concentrate on the road.

The light was red, so I reluctantly slowed down. Just as I approached the intersection, the light turned green. I dropped the transmission into second, dumped the clutch, and proceeded to gun it, only to be T-boned by a large pickup truck speeding through the red light. I let out a cry to Heaven, "JESUSSSSSSSSSSSSSSSSS!!!!!!!!" as I saw a huge grill and a blurry blue Ford oval smash right into my car. I heard Gary call out my name. "JASON!!! BABES!!!" There were puffs of white smoke that filled the passenger cabin. My body and face were enveloped by the airbags doing their part to keep the truck from violently trespassing further into the driver's side of my car. My skin began to sting. All of a sudden, I felt light headed as if on an amusement park ride exerting way too many G-forces. I felt the car spin around a few times. With each violent spin the car encountered, images of Gary, Michael, my mom, my baby sister and niece, flashed in front of me before the car came to rest around a telephone pole on the corner of the street. The last image was that of my dad. It was the clearest of them all. I could see every beautiful detail, every feature, and every imperfection in his pleasant face. The first words he ever spoke to me were revealed in that instant and resonated loud and strong in my ears, "Hold on, son!" I was a bouncing baby boy all of a sudden. My tiny right hand latched on to a couple of his fingers, as I steadied myself on the hard wood floor taking my first steps in the comfort of my parents first home in Detroit. I saw myself focusing on my footing and gaining confidence from the motivating influence of my dad. His face was awash with a father's love. I tried to move towards him wondering if I was dying while a fire ignited from under the hood of the car. The flames were the last real image I saw before slipping out of consciousness. They were indicative of the proud light illuminating from His face, shining bright as he vehemently admonished me to, *"Hold on, son!...*